A SCI-FI ALI

A TALLEAN MATES NOVELLA

LYNNEA LEE

Copyright © 2021 Lynnea Lee

All rights reserved

The characters and events portrayed in this book are fictitious. Any similarity to real persons, living or dead, is coincidental and not intended by the author.

No part of this book may be reproduced, or stored in a retrieval system, or transmitted in any form or by any means, electronic, mechanical, photocopying, recording, or otherwise, without express written permission of the publisher.

ISBN: 9798532386815

Cover design by: Kasmit Covers

CHAPTER 1

Kajar couldn't take his eyes off the human female on the auction block. She was calm and collected, even regal, despite the fact she was almost naked and paraded around like a piece of meat. He'd never had a thing for human females, but he knew in an instant he would not leave the planet without her on his ship.

According to the auctioneer, the female only had one previous owner. From the muscles on her arms and legs, her strong shoulders, and healthy curves, her previous owner had treated her well. She'd been fed well and was in the prime of her health. The fire still burned strong in her dark eyes. This was no broken slave; she'd been a pet.

She looked down at her bidders through a curtain of thick, shiny black hair, as if challenging them to raise the price as high as possible. She knew the more they paid for her, the more likely she would be treated well, like a trophy rather than a workhorse.

The female smiled at someone in the audience, and Kajar followed her gaze to a fat, pompous merchant, covered in so many fancy accessories, Kajar wondered how he moved at all. It was a smart move for the female to catch his eye; being a part of Yanus' ever-growing harem was much preferable to many other options.

Yanus had already won the previous human female on the stand and had a harem of them waiting at home. Why in the galaxy would he need more? The male had a fetish for the exotic females and had a stronghold somewhere filled with an army of them, bored to death, doing nothing but look pretty and fight for his affections. Kajar hated him on principle.

With Yanus and a lesser-known Dominion captain bidding on the female, her price shot up ridiculously fast. Many of the others interested had given up, but the two still dueled, pushing the profits ever higher.

Kajar couldn't afford her. Even her starting bid had been surprisingly high, probably because of her health and vitality. He wouldn't ever pay for a slave anyway. It was against everything he believed in.

While he wasn't one to buy a slave, acquiring one through any means possible was a definite possibility. He didn't care if he had to spend a small fortune on distractions to get her onto his ship, as long as the credits never reached Dominion hands.

Kajar knew who'd win: Yanus. The merchant had only started spending, and he had a lot more credits at his disposal than the captain. As the bidding price increased, the captain began hesitating before raising each bid.

Kajar started working on a plan.

The merchant raised the price again, and, this time, the captain waited for the last moment to speak, his voice lacking the certainty it had just a minute earlier. Predicting the result, Kajar left the auction and got to work. This beautiful female would go to Yanus, the human hoarder—except she wouldn't. She'd go home with Kajar.

Kajar's first step was to figure out a way to distract the merchant so he wouldn't check on his new prize for a while. Easy. He'd just have to make sure Yanus knew all about the blonde-haired beauty the auction house had saved for last. Who better to do the job than the employees themselves? The more credits the auction house made, the more they paid their attendants for the day. It encouraged the workers to push the wares.

He stood right behind a pair of attendants and mumbled to another patron, "Stars. I wonder how much that merchant would bid on the blonde female if he's bidding this much for the one up there now. Can you imagine the bonuses the house will give out at the end of the night?"

"I heard Yanus has a thing for females with light hair," the patron replied back. It was common knowledge.

The pair of auction house employees, having overheard their talk, inched toward Yanus, eager to remind him of the blonde up for grabs at the end of the night.

Next, he needed the attendants cleared from the area where winners of the auction picked up their new possessions. He wasn't stupid enough to steal from the powerfully rich merchant in his own vehicle or with a hired one, so Kajar planned on driving right up with his "borrowed" transport and getting his new female into the back. Since he was at the auction looking for things to commandeer—he hated the word steal—he'd arrived in a "borrowed" vehicle, so he was already ahead of the game.

Clearing the attendants was also easily accomplished. No one passed up free food, especially if they thought it was given out by the company they worked for. Ordering a large amount of food to the location was still nowhere near a fraction of the price Yanus would pay for the female.

It was common for either the auction house or happy auction winners to order food for the workers, and it wouldn't be suspicious at all. Besides, no employee would admit they'd left their watch and let a precious commodity be stolen because of free food. Not unless they wanted to lose their job. They would make up some emergency instead and back each other up.

Finally, he needed the keys to her room. Another

simple task. The merchant would have it in his possession in a few short moments after he made the winning bid. And Kajar happened to be an exceptional pickpocket, something he picked up as a young male to survive on his own.

He'd always been on his own. The only thing his sire had left for him was his ship. He'd been young when the Dominion took his parents away. He'd never quite figured out the whole story, only that he was alone now. He would have given anything to have his parents back, but a ship was all he'd gotten.

He'd learned to make it on his own since then, but not always by honest means. The first few years had been tough. He did well for himself now and had even upgraded the old craft with the newest technology. He lived comfortably and didn't have to fall back on illegal activities often. Kajar trusted no one and needed no one except himself, but it was a lonely existence.

Today that would change. In just a few hours, he would have a female in his arms, and the galaxy would be theirs for the taking.

❃ ❃ ❃

Anna sat on the couch waiting for her new

owner. A merchant. She'd finally gotten lucky again. Throughout the entire bidding, she'd prayed for the merchant to win. Every human slave had heard of how many merchants had developed obsessions for their human females, doting on them and spoiling them, and her old owner had told her the same. It was a much better choice than the Dominion captain.

She'd been on a Dominion ship before on her way here and never ever wanted to be on one again. She'd stayed quiet in the back the whole trip to the auction house, and been lucky none of the officers had paid attention to her. Some of the other women hadn't been so lucky.

This wasn't her first rodeo. She'd been on the auction block once before and had phenomenal luck that time too. She'd been purchased by an elderly couple who needed help around the house. They'd treated her well and even had plans in place for her to go to a friend after they were gone, but things didn't work out that way.

Since the couple's deaths, Anna had run into some horrible luck. On her way to her new home, her new owner had gotten himself arrested for some crime or another. They'd thrown her on a Dominion ship to the first available auction. It had been a grueling trip; the conditions of the ship were so bad she could almost hear her late owners yelling at the guards for putting her in such horrid conditions. Now, here she was, standing on the pedestal again.

Her luck had started to change, though. The auction house had set her starting bid high, and she'd caught the eyes of the most garishly dressed merchant she'd ever seen. That was a good sign. She'd also caught the eyes of a Dominion captain—not so good; they were known to get violent. Some merchants abused their slaves, but her chances were still better with him. She'd sent the merchant her most alluring smile.

Between the two of them, her bids rose past the numbers establishments like pleasure houses were willing to pay, and she was out of the red zone. The merchant had won in the end.

Now, after a long wait, the door finally opened. She expected to see the slightly pudgy face of the gaudily dressed merchant, but instead, a stranger walked in. A hood covered his face, and he was built lean and muscular—definitely not her merchant.

"Who are you?" she demanded.

The stranger looked around at the corners of the room before pulling off his hood. Bright yellow-green eyes met hers, and for a moment all she could do was gawk at the gorgeous face revealed from under the hood. He was like a GQ model but alien, with the telltale cheek creases and angular face structure of his species. Like all Talleans, his skin was like soft-textured leather, adding ruggedness to his devilish good looks.

He grinned, the points of his fangs showing. "You are just as feisty as you look. I love it! I'm here for you." Her translator did its work, but she could tell from the way he talked he had a different accent than the other Talleans she'd met. The Tallean language had sounded like a series of growls to her at first, but it had been years since she'd been taken from Earth, and she could now differentiate the words.

"I was won by a merchant."

"You were. But I've decided you are coming with me instead." He stepped in close and pulled her up from the couch and into his arms.

She gasped. "What? Am I getting kidnapped?"

"You are no child." He looked her up and down. "No child at all. I'm freeing you so you may travel the stars with me."

"No, no, no. This isn't happening." She shook her head. "I finally have the good luck to be bought by a merchant—you know, the ones most likely to fall in love with me and give me a good life—and I get stolen?"

"Stolen? No, I like to call it... liberation."

"Fuck this. I'm not going to let my good luck go to waste. Merchant, or thief? I'll take my chances with the merchant." She opened her mouth to scream.

A large hand covered it. "Don't you dare! I went through a lot of trouble to distract that bloated, overstuffed merchant and the attendants to get to you."

Keeping his hand over her mouth, he maneuvered

her to the door.

Crap! He was going to take her whether she wanted him to or not. She gestured wildly toward her only piece of luggage. It was everything she owned and was supposed to come with her. She was wearing a see-through gown meant to entice the best buyer, and her real clothes were inside the small case. And the photo. She didn't have any reminders of Earth, but she had a photo of herself and the couple who had kept her for the past few years.

Sure, they had bought her, but they had also given her the best life she'd ever had. Having grown up in foster care, being bounced from house to house—she couldn't even call them homes—it was the first instance of stability she'd ever known.

"The announcer did say you came with your own belongings." He moved them over to the case, hand still over her mouth. "Grab it, and let's go."

He pulled his hood tightly over his face again so that his features were cast in shadow. He moved Anna over to the door, opened it a crack, and poked his head outside. Then he pulled her out, stuffed her into a transport waiting just outside, and closed the door behind her.

Anna pushed and pulled at the door handle, but the transport didn't give. Moments later, the door to the front opened, and her kidnapper slid into the driver's seat. Unlike the other transports she'd been inside, this one used a live driver. Was it his personal vehicle? Stealing from an auction house with a personal vehicle? This guy was either stupid or had balls of steel.

She held her luggage to her chest as the auction house disappeared behind them.

CHAPTER 2

Kajar rechecked the lock to the room before looking outside the window. It seemed they'd gotten to the inn without detection. The merchant probably didn't even know she was gone yet. He was most likely trying to outbid the other buyers for the pretty blonde.

"Scream all you want. Everyone will just think you are a bad slave in need of some discipline."

He took his hand off her mouth and glowered at her, daring her to try screaming again. Instead, she snapped her teeth at his fingers. He snatched them away just in time.

"Ooh, bitey. You got any more fetishes I should know about?"

The female glared daggers at him, looking downright adorable. She was still upset about being taken from the auction house. She seemed adamant about going home with the merchant. Why? He didn't understand.

"I'd like to have you know that Yanus was late picking you up because another pretty Earth female has caught his eye. He bought the human female before you, the one with the red hair, and he stayed behind to wait for the blonde. If you were looking for some merchant to fall in love with you, it wasn't him. Yanus loves Earth females; all of them. I—" he sent her his sexiest smile, "—only want you." He tapped the tip of her nose and had to avoid her snapping teeth again.

She scrunched her nose at his words. "The words of a thief."

"I don't pay for intelligent lives."

"You just steal them."

"Liberate," he corrected.

"Okay, so I was to be a part of a harem, so what? That doesn't sound bad when my other options are pleasure houses and sadistic Dominion captains."

"You have another option now. You can travel with me. I'll provide for you."

"Whatever." She stomped over to the facilities carrying her bag along.

That had gone better than planned. The female hadn't screamed, yelled at, bitten him—successfully —or even cried. Kajar considered that a bonus.

He ordered a meal for them since he doubted she'd had the opportunity to eat all day.

She came out of the facilities wearing a set of

comfortable lounge clothes. These were not the clothes of a slave; they looked like quality goods. Kajar leaned in to take a better look. He reached out and touched the silky fabric of the loose pants.

"Ever heard of personal space?"

That didn't sound like a slave talking either. Kajar had made a great choice; he wouldn't need to undo any unwanted Dominion slave training. "These look expensive."

She shrugged.

"Was that why you were sending that beautiful smile of yours over to that fat merchant, princess?"

She frowned at the nickname, and he frowned back just thinking about her catching the eyes of some stuffy merchant with more credits than he could ever use.

"Were you owned by a merchant before?"

The auction had not given the details of her previous owner.

"No." She suddenly looked sad. "I wasn't. I was sending him that smile because Jola told me to. "

"Jola. That sounds Tallean."

"Jola and Kortas were my owners. They died recently."

Sadness was a strange reaction for an Earthling talking about her previous owners.

"Jola and Kortas arranged to send me to a friend after they passed. He was supposed to take care of me, but the idiot got himself arrested while I was in transit, and they shunted me back into the system. What else is new?" She blew out a frustrated breath. "Kortas didn't think I'd ever need the advice, but Jola insisted. She told me if I ever ended up on the auction block again to stand tall and proud and catch the attention of a merchant. They'd also inflated my worth in their will in case I ended up on the block again, so I'd end up in a good place."

"No wonder your bid started so high."

"Jola must be rolling in her grave right now—getting stolen by a thief."

"Liber—" He cut the word short at her glare. "Just pretend I'm the male Jola and Kortas meant for you to go to. I will care for you."

She looked at him warily, but he bulldozed ahead.

"I'm Kajar. What's your name?"

"Anna."

Anna. The name seemed almost too simple for someone as intriguing as her.

A knock came at the door, and Kajar moved Anna out of sight before opening the door for their food, taking a chance on her not trying to escape.

"Come eat." He sat and pulled the other chair right next to him so they could share the tray of food. Secretly he also wanted her as close to him as possible. "See, I can provide too. You don't need a stuffy merchant with a harem of human females he probably doesn't even remember the names of."

"Fine, I'll give you a chance. That is, if you don't get caught by law enforcement first." She came and plopped down in the seat next to him, the soft fabric covering her thighs brushing against him.

"Me? Get caught? Never been caught in my life." He puffed out his chest much like a youngster impressing a female. He'd gotten very close to getting caught many times, but he wasn't going to tell her that. He wanted her to have faith in him.

For someone like him, getting caught once was the end. He didn't have a crew to break him out. He didn't have anyone to even look for him. Now that he had Anna, he would have to be even more careful. He didn't want to leave her alone.

"Ha! So you admit you hide from the law often."

"Never said I didn't."

Not knowing what she liked, he'd ordered a meat wrap: a food that most people, even youngsters, enjoyed. She picked up the wrap in her tiny hands, and the thing looked positively enormous. She tilted it one way and then the other, trying to get her mouth around it. It was adorable.

Kajar stifled a laugh but broke into a huge smile instead.

"It's not funny. Who makes wraps this size?" She nibbled on the cut edge, managing a small bite of the shell and the filling.

"If you're having trouble with that, how are you going to wrap your lips around my—"

"Don't even go there." She shot him an offended look, and he laughed.

Seeing that he was taking things lightly, she relaxed.

He picked up the other half and took a big bite, showing her how it was done.

"Easy for you. You have a big mouth!"

※ ※ ※

Anna looked through her lashes at the Tallean thief who'd kidnapped her. He hadn't done anything to hurt her yet, and he didn't seem the type to do so. He'd said he refused to pay for a life, and he did use words like "liberate" and "free" to describe his theft of her. Those were good signs, right?

Of course, she didn't know if he had a bad temper. Even the nicest guys could become monsters when angry.

She took another bite of the meaty wrap. Back in the transport, when he'd mentioned bringing her to an inn, she'd imagined a dingy little motel. This place was actually pretty nice. It was more like a 5-star hotel than an inn. And the food was great too. He clearly wasn't hurting for credits.

Maybe she could have a decent life with him. You know, before shit happened again and she got moved around to her next home. While she'd wanted to go home with the merchant because he'd been the best choice there, Anna wasn't particularly attached to the idea.

She'd learned throughout her life not to get attached to much. Her years with her late owners had been the longest she'd ever stayed in one place since she could remember. Now they were gone too.

Merchant, thief. Who cared who owned her? As long as they weren't abusive, she'd take it.

Kajar at least paid attention to her, unlike some of the homes she'd been in. He'd noticed the quality of her clothes. They were the nicest things she'd ever owned. Everything in that bag was. Jola and Kortas never had offspring, having met later in life. They also had more savings than they could ever use on themselves, so they'd bought her nice things.

They'd only allowed her to keep the one bag she had on her body when they transferred her to the Dominion ship. Luckily, she wasn't attached to items either.

And Kajar's first reaction was to feed her, not to take advantage of her. Sure he'd made a lewd joke about her going down on him, but the way he'd said it wasn't menacing. He'd been teasing.

Maybe her bad luck was really over.

She took one last bite of her side of the wrap and

put it back on the tray. "I'm stuffed. This thing is huge."

"Stuffed? Not yet. But don't you worry, I'll take good care of you." Kajar barely kept from laughing at his own horribly tasteless joke. He waggled his brows at her exaggeratedly.

She rolled her eyes. She wasn't just stuck with a thief; she was stuck with an immature one who thought he was funny. Great. "So what else do you do besides stealing damsels in distress?"

"I try to take as many legitimate jobs as I can, but I still do some…commandeering occasionally. Especially if I believe credits shouldn't exchange hands for the items, and then only from the Dominion. I had no choice when I was younger."

She looked at his perfectly sculpted face. "Are you not young now?"

"I was barely grown when I started living on my own and running my ship."

Another orphan like her? Or a runaway? Did it matter?

"A ship. So you don't live on New Rhea?"

Duh! She realized what a silly question that was the moment it left her mouth. They were at an inn. If he lived here, wouldn't he have brought her home?

"I travel between the outer planets, finding odd jobs here and there. Sometimes it's a delivery job. Other times it's to get information. And of course, I sell whatever I commandeer."

He avoided the word steal like the plague.

"It's a living. And I get to make my own hours and direct my own life. I'm in space often, and I move from planet to planet. I like it like that."

"So it's just you and your crew most of the time."

He grimaced. "I work alone. No crew. I don't need one. I liberated you and got away, didn't I?"

"You *think* you got away. How do you know the guy who paid for me isn't on your tail right now?" She looked out the window and noticed many of the port's law enforcement milling around below their eighth-story window. "Like those guys there. How do you know they aren't here for you? For me?"

Kajar stood, looked out the window, and frowned.

"Fuck! He *is* on my tail. They must have tracked the transport here." He pulled them back away from the window. "They couldn't have tracked us to this room though. This inn has no internal cameras, and no one could bribe the employees to give up the footage. Their privacy policy is their best selling point. But there's nothing stopping them from checking every single room until they find us. Law enforcement on this planet could just use brute force. That's why I prefer the wilds and space."

Kajar took the unfinished wrap from the tray and polished it off in a few large bites.

"It's time we get out of here."

"If they're looking for me, isn't it dangerous to leave the room?"

"Yeah, if you shout it to the world. Are you going to work with me, or do you still want to be part of some rich merchant's harem? I can't offer you a life of idle boredom, but I can give you excitement and freedom in spades. And I promise to protect you."

Anna had never been given a choice before. Freedom and a life to explore the planets sounded better than being bored to death as part of a harem. "Didn't you say you've never gotten caught?"

"Never."

She grinned back at Kajar, making her choice. "Then what are you waiting for? Let's get out of here!"

CHAPTER 3

Kajar led the little human female through the hallways to the service elevator at the back of the building. He'd stolen the keys from the cleaning staff last time he was here and made a copy before giving it back to the front desk, claiming he'd found it outside his door. He'd already checked it yesterday and knew it still worked.

The elevator would lead them down to the back end of the inn, where the laundry and kitchens were. The staff had a separate entrance to the building. If they were lucky, there wouldn't be any officers posted there.

Anna lugged her sole piece of luggage into the elevator with her. It was a small bag but still bulky on her frame. She was fit and strong but still much smaller than him. He took the bag and tied it to his own pack, using the straps to keep it from moving around.

"You shouldn't need to carry my bag," she protested.

"I want to." With her hands freed, he took her hand in his and held it. "So I could do this."

She smiled, and the whole dreary elevator lit up as if by a million stars. This wasn't the fake smile she'd sent to the merchant while on the auction block. This was genuine.

As if pulled toward her by an invisible force, Kajar leaned down and pressed his nose against the side of her head, nuzzling her temple. She froze as if she'd never been touched before. But a gorgeous female like her? Impossible! She smelled good too, like the first breath of fresh air after months on his ship.

He slid his fingers through the dark silky strands of her hair, grabbing a handful as she tilted her head up to him. She closed her eyes and pressed her cheek against his face but did not return the nuzzling. He dragged his lips over her smooth, crease-free cheek, enjoying the softness of her skin.

The elevator dinged, signaling the ground floor, and Kajar lifted his head reluctantly. She stared back at him with round eyes.

Still holding her hand, he led her through the twists and turns of the inn's inner workings and made his way to the back door. A few workers gave them odd looks, but no one stopped them.

"Stay right here. I need to check to make sure they don't have anyone waiting outside." He left her by the door, away from sight.

He picked up a uniform top from a cart and threw it over his head. His black pants would blend into the background. To anyone searching, he would look like an employee taking a break. He stepped out and glanced around. The coast was clear.

He ducked back in, tore the top off, and grabbed Anna's hands in his again.

"Just walk next to me and act normal."

She nodded, and her hands tightened around his.

They stepped out into the alleyway and crossed it before ducking right back inside, this time into the back of the shopping complex next door. They wove through the back hallways of the complex and exited out into the main shopping area.

Hopefully, they blended in with the other shoppers. They should look like a slave and her owner, albeit one that doted on his coveted possession a bit much, what with her expensive-looking lounge wear and him holding her hand. But that wasn't a rare sight anymore, especially on New Rhea.

The Dominion elites frowned on cross-species pairings, preferring to think of humans as subpar and not compatible for mating for the Tallean species. The elites called themselves the Chosen of the Goddess and even considered the average Talleans too lowly and crude for the likes of them. They would never sully their genes with anyone with inferior genetics.

But New Rhea was on the edge of Dominion territory, and the rules were more relaxed out here. Kajar often saw mixed couples in the ports.

They wove through the shopping complex, pretending to be just another mixed couple, before exiting the shopping complex on the far side. No law enforcement met them.

"We need to go by foot." He looked down at her feet and frowned. "Pink bejeweled slippers?" He hadn't noticed them before. "You can't trek in the wilderness with those, princess. We are going to leave the port."

"Stop calling me that," she huffed. "You stole me as a slave from an auction house. So what if I have a few nice things? They're all I ever owned."

Kajar put his hands up in a universal sign of surrender. He'd been annoyed that she'd preferred the rich merchant over him at first and had let it color his words. Anna had picked him in the end, and he should let it go.

"What about your transport?" she asked as she pulled a pair of closed-toe shoes out from her bag. It was a good thing she had them. All Tallean footwear were open at the front to let out their claws, even the boots. They would've had a hard time finding something that would protect her human feet on a moment's notice.

"They probably have footage of the transport leaving the auction house. Lucky for us, that transport isn't mine." He helped her keep her balance, and she changed her shoes and stuffed the slippers back into her bag.

"Did you steal that too?"

"Borrowed. And I left it in good condition. I'm not dumb enough to liberate a slave in my own transport." He took her hand in his again and led her toward the edge of the port.

"I'm sorry we have to walk. I don't trust the hired transport not to recognize your face from the auction house photo."

"I can handle it, even in my pink slippers."

"I know you can." He smirked. "Princess."

She snapped at him again with her teeth, and he bellowed a laugh. Damn, she was a feisty thing!

✷ ✷ ✷

The feeling of excitement surged through Anna as they left the hubbub of the port and headed into the quieter residential areas on the outskirts. New Rhea was nothing like the inner planet she'd been on previously.

The inner planet cities were polished and high-tech, at least in the area where she'd lived. Jola and Kortas had been well-off, and their neighborhood had been clean and pristine. Anna had never left that perfect section of town. Every place she'd needed to go to run her errands had been nearby.

Four times a day, a bell would ring, and every resident would drop to their knees in prayer to the Goddess. Jola had warned her to get down on her knees as soon as she heard the bell, lest the guards and officers punish her for being slow in her worship of the Goddess.

Back at the edge of the port, a similar bell had rung, and she'd dropped to her knees automatically through her conditioning. Then she'd realized that Kajar stood through the prayers, as did many of the other Talleans. Only a few dropped to their knees as she did.

Unlike the long prayers in the inner planets, the prayers on New Rhea were short. Barely ten seconds had gone by, and everyone was back to whatever they were doing. It was as if the bell and prayers were only cursory, just so people could say they did them.

Kajar had frowned at her. "There's no need for that with me. I don't believe in the Goddess."

Anna had stared at him wide-eyed that he'd dared speak such blasphemy. Then she'd peered around, worried someone had heard. The elites would make an example out of him. But he'd just laughed.

"They are not as strict out here. Don't worry. There won't be armed males hunting my heathen ass down."

Anna had finally relaxed when none came. "What do you believe in then?"

Kajar had tilted his head to the sky. "My parents believed in the Stars."

"But not you?"

"You are the first good thing the Stars have brought me. I'm undecided."

Heat rose to Anna's face at his words, but he didn't notice. He just kept moving forward.

Things were different here. The whole area lacked the high-tech, polished feel. Back at the port where the auction house and hotel had been, the buildings were ruggedly built and had an industrial quality to them. Now that they'd left the central hub and walked into a residential area, the buildings had a certain rustic charm.

"You look like you've never seen houses before."

"This is so different from the place where I lived. The area of town I lived in had sleek grey and white buildings with metal and glass. Everything was clean and shiny. And cookie-cutter. This place looks —" she searched for the word "—homey. Charming. Every house is different."

"Probably because the settlers built their own homes when they arrived. You were probably on one of the inner planets, in the nice part of a city. I've never been, but I've seen photos. I've also seen images of their slums."

Anna had heard about the slums but had never

seen them.

"Past these houses are the wild areas."

"Wait, that's it? We've only been walking for a while." She'd thought it would take a few hours of trekking to get out into the wilds, but they'd only been walking for maybe an hour at most, though she had no idea how long hours were on this planet.

"This is the smallest port on the planet, and they crowd everything into a small footprint. The shopping complex we were in is a dozen stories high. We are lucky we are already at the edge of town. They are probably done checking all the rooms by now and are most likely spreading out around the port to find us. I bet they've found the borrowed vehicle and know we are on foot."

Anna was enjoying herself so much she'd almost forgotten they were on the run. This wasn't just some leisurely stroll through a charming town. "Where exactly are we going? And what's the plan?"

"I've got a hideout just outside of town. We'll bunk down for the night and wait for them to give up. Then we can circle back in and head to my ship. Yanus doesn't live here, and he'll need to go home eventually with the rest of the females he bought. Once he's gone, no one will care about a single missing slave."

"That actually sounds like a good plan."

"Of course it is. Remember, I've never gotten caught." He sent her that panty-wetting grin again, the lopsided one that showed a sexy fang on one side.

It reminded her of what had happened in the elevator. Kajar had nuzzled her. It was the Talleans' version of a kiss, and instead of nuzzling back, Anna had frozen, surprised at the effect it had on her body.

Even now, as she thought of Kajar leaving his kisses across her cheeks, her face heated and turned red. Her heartbeat sped up, and a tingling started in her belly and spread down to the V of her legs. She took smaller steps, worried Kajar would scent her arousal. Talleans had a phenomenal sense of smell, and she knew arousal and fear were the easiest to detect.

If he did know of her thoughts, he didn't show it.

Instead, he led them through the houses quickly until they came to a high wall.

Anna gawked at the barrier. She hadn't known the port and the surrounding homes were walled-in. Was it to keep citizens in or creatures out? She didn't like it either way.

"Why do they need to wall off the port?"

"It's there to make everyone feel safe. Many of the outer planets wall off their cities. New Rhea's wildlife isn't as dangerous as the ones on Vosthea or Reka 5, but there are a few vicious predators, and residents like to feel protected."

"And you're taking me out there?"

"I've spent a lot of time out in the wilds on many

of the outer planets. The walls are to protect those ignorant of the dangers and lacking the skills to survive." He stopped in front of a door in the wall and fished around his bag for his large ring of key tabs.

"How did you get all the keys? First the hotel service elevator key, now this one. This doesn't seem like a key most people living here would have. Besides, you said you don't even live here."

"I made copies of the originals and then snuck them back to their owners. This key I got by getting a guard black-out drunk after his shift. That cost me more than I want to remember in Rhean spirits." He held the key to the lock pad, pushed the door open, and stepped through.

Anna hesitated, unsure what she would find beyond the walls.

Kajar held out his hand, his trouble-maker grin ever-present. "I'll protect you. I promise."

CHAPTER 4

Kajar carefully sliced the thick, thorny vine off of Anna's legs with the claws of his feet. The claws came in handy when traversing the wild. Then he knelt to pick off the sharp spikes and brambles that had embedded themselves in Anna's silky pants.

She'd tried to ignore them at first, but this last set of burrs were still attached firmly to the original plant and had tripped her up.

"Thanks, Kajar. I wish I had claws on my feet like you right now. I'm not dressed for this trip, am I? For some reason, I expected some tamed woodland. This place is horrible. Everything latches on and sticks and itches."

Kajar had brought them through this door, right into a patch of brambles, on purpose. If anyone were following them, they would have to traverse these annoying plants too. Also, later on, there was a patch of carrion plants; they would remove any ability to follow their scent.

"Do you have tighter pants you can change into?"

Anna looked disappointed. "No. Wide legs are the current trend on the inner planets, and that's all I have. Unless I wear shorts, which is probably a worse idea."

Her legs would be all scratched up. That was not acceptable.

"We should have picked up something more utilitarian for you back at the shopping complex." Kajar removed the last of the troublesome branches and sheathed his knife. He threw the offending mess into the brush before sweeping Anna into his arms.

She squeaked and threw her arms around his neck.

"I'll carry you until we are through this patch."

"Thank you."

Anna didn't release her arms and instead kept them tight around his neck. Kajar didn't mind. He enjoyed her body pressed up against him, and he loved that she trusted him to care for her.

They stepped around the remains of an animal unlucky enough to be trapped in the brambles. Without the dexterity of hands and a brain to untangle itself, the animal had gotten trapped and starved. Its body would feed the next season of brambles.

"Poor thing. Damn, Nature, you a bitch."

"I would rather deal with nature than with society," Kajar admitted. "Nature is consistent. Learn the rules, play by them, and survive. Nature always has the upper hand, but at least it doesn't cheat or lie."

"And how do you not die when you're still learning the rules?"

"I admit, I had help in the beginning. When the Dominion came for my parents, I inherited their ship. It kept me mobile and gave me a place to stay. But it was my sire's journal that kept me fed and alive."

"A journal?"

"He documented a lot of the wildlife and plants on the outer planets, including which ones were edible, which ones were poisonous, and which ones were useful. I keep a copy with me at all times, even though I've memorized it all by now."

"Was he some kind of bushman?"

"More like an amateur biologist. That's why he had his ship, so he could go around and document everything. I remember spending a lot of time out in the forests with them before the Dominion took them in."

"I'm sorry you lost them."

"Don't be. It was a long time ago."

Kajar had never told anyone of his sire's journal. He'd never had anyone to tell. He had many acquaintances but no friends. The only males he saw more than once every galactic year were Jakkan and his crew. Jakkan posed as a rich merchant while in the inner planets, even going by another name. But Jakkan and his crew were just as secretive as Kajar. They were closer to business associates, since they often paid him to help release Earth-made goods from Dominion hands.

It was refreshing to have someone here. Someone intelligent and brave and willing to trek out into the forest with him, even if she wasn't dressed for the occasion.

At the edge of the brambles, a smell hit them.

"Ugh! What the heck is that?" Anna made a gagging sound and burrowed her nose into his shirt.

"Ready for the next lesson?"

She replied with another retching sound, and Kajar put her down on her feet.

"That patch over there has carrion plants." He pointed to the inconspicuous patch with little red flowers.

"They look so normal, but they stink like the devil's armpit. Yuck!"

"They don't just stink. They mess up our ability to follow a scent. Now that I've breathed it in, I won't be able to track anything I'm hunting."

She nodded in understanding. "And anyone following us won't be able to track us either. That's pretty smart!"

Kajar grinned at her, and she grimaced, unable to smile through the horrible stench.

"My hideout is close by. It's just out of the range of

the carrion plants."

He guided her away from the odorous patch and toward a densely forested area. The entrance to the cave would be overgrown by brush by now. He hadn't used this location for over a year, preferring to have many hideouts scattered across different planets.

He needed to hack a pathway in for them. He took out the larger curved blade from his pack and took off his hooded jacket. Then, he started clearing the brush, hacking away at the overgrowth of greenery. The goal was to make a path just big enough but not obvious to untrained eyes.

Kajar felt Anna's eyes on his shoulders and back as he worked, and the unmistakable scent of her arousal filled the forest air.

✼ ✼ ✼

Anna couldn't look away from the tempting sea of rippling muscles as Kajar whacked away at the brush with his machete-like blade. This alien male in front of her wasn't just fit and ridiculously well-built; he was capable and knowledgeable. His body wasn't made in a gym; it was the result of years of hard work and survival.

The way he moved as if he knew precisely what he was doing was a big turn-on. Some guys talked the talk, but Kajar was the real deal. He was capable and strong.

Anna doubted that merchant could do half the things Kajar could do, and she knew in her heart of hearts she'd made the right choice. She was in competent hands, and she didn't need to share with a harem of other females.

Kajar was genuinely kind to her, treating her like a person and not a thing to be owned. He was patient as well. He'd carried her through the brambles and didn't once blame her for being unprepared for the wilderness.

He swung the blade a few more times, clearing a hole barely big enough for himself in the brush, before wiping off his brow with the back of his hand. Even sweaty, the guy was hot, and Anna wanted to be under his body and covered in his sweat. Which, if it were anyone else, would be kind of gross, but Kajar was…Kajar. And Anna was starting to crush on the guy hard.

He tucked the blade back into his pack, making sure to keep the sharp edge covered. Then he held out a hand to her. Anna resisted the urge to titter like a school girl and took it, following him into the brush.

The cleared pathway ended at the mouth of a cave. There was just enough of a glow coming through the brush to illuminate a few feet into it, but the rest was dark except for a column of light shining from the ceiling of the cave farther in.

Kajar squeezed her hand, and they ducked into the cave. He sat her down on some sort of seat and released her fingers to fish around in his pack. She missed his touch immediately. He brought out a tiny lantern and turned it on, bathing the walls with dim light. Kajar really was prepared for everything.

"I'll need to start a fire to dry out the cave a bit. The wet season just ended, and everything is damp." He dug in his pack again and brought a roll of synthetic cord and a flask that he tied around his hips with the cord. Then he handed her his comm. "Look through this and watch our supplies while I'm gone. I need to secure the perimeter and gather some dry fuel for a fire." He jerked his thumb at the pile of wood stacked in the corner of the cave. "That's too damp to use."

Anna looked down at the comm unit in her hand. Drawings of the plants she'd seen on their trek stared back at her from the screen. "This is a copy of your father's journal."

Kajar put his hand over hers and scrolled the screen from side to side, showing the different pages. Anna's skin tingled where they touched, and she wished he didn't need to leave the cave but understood.

"Thank you for sharing this. This is something special."

"I'll be back soon. I won't venture far. You'll be safe

here."

Then he pulled her to his body and held her to his chest, nuzzling the top of her head. This time, instead of freezing, she acted. She tilted her chin and kissed whatever she could reach, which happened to be his rugged jawline.

Talleans didn't kiss mouth to mouth, and Anna wondered what his reaction would be. She wrapped her arms around his neck and pulled his lips to hers. She kissed him lightly, waiting to see his response. It only took him a moment before he devoured her mouth with his.

His fingers tangled in her hair possessively as his other hand reached down to secure her hip. His mouth left hers and trailed down her throat; his hand in her hair tilted her head and exposed her throat to him. He buried his face there and inhaled deeply.

He pulled away from her reluctantly with a low growl. "The sun will set soon, and I must hurry to secure our hideout." Then he was gone, leaving her lusting for more.

Kajar was right. The sun did set soon. It only felt like a moment after he left when the light shining in from outside dimmed, and Anna was left with just the light of the lantern and the comm unit. She tried to focus on the screen and the plants and animals described there, but every noise in the forest, every crack of a branch or rustle of leaves, sent her mind on a terrifying journey of what-ifs.

She was glad she had the comm with all the drawings. Many of the journal entries were of innocuous small shrew-like or lizard-like animals. Many of the plants were listed as poisonous—she'd learned the Tallean glyph for that in her few years with her previous owners. Her ability to read the Tallean language was limited but words like "poisonous," "danger," "eats plants," or "good to eat" stuck out to her, and she made sense of the rest the best she could.

There were many plants labeled poisonous, but not many animals listed with the word danger. That was a good sign. She told herself to stop imagining a saber tooth tiger every time something rustled beyond the mouth of the cave.

There was one bird that looked absolutely terrifying. It was a ground-dwelling bird that looked like a cross between a vulture and a shoebill stork—one of those prehistoric dinosaur-looking ones. The drawn image showed it tearing into a carcass. Anna hoped she wouldn't bump into one anytime soon, or at all.

A screeching sound echoed outside the cave, and Anna looked around nervously. She picked up the lantern, held it in front of her body, and peered around it, trying to make out any shapes outside. More unidentified sounds came from the darkness, and goosebumps crawled up her arm.

Then came another sound, an ominous *tick-tick-tick* that made her skin crawl.

She wasn't sure, but it sounded like it came from just outside the cave. Anna resisted the temptation to call out and ask if it was Kajar. She'd seen too many scary movies in her life and knew better than to give herself away.

She sure hoped Kajar was safe and got back soon; she was a sitting duck in here.

CHAPTER 5

Kajar had ended up leaving Anna for longer than he wanted. But, he'd managed to not only set a perimeter alarm and refill his flask at the river—the water in the pool closer to his hideout was not potable—but also set some traps and snares.

He had some nutrition bars in his pack, but when he'd left for the auction house this morning, he hadn't expected an extended camping trip. He'd brought everything he needed in case he wound up hiding in the woods, but he hadn't expected to have another person to care for.

Lucky for them, the forest around the port didn't have many dangerous animals. There was one large, land-bound bird that had the hardware to be dangerous, but it mostly fed off the dead, choosing to let others make the kill for it. It didn't actually hunt unless it was desperate, usually at the tail end of the dry season when food was scarce.

However, the area boasted plenty of poisonous and obnoxious plants. As long as Anna stayed in the cave, she wouldn't accidentally bump into or ingest any of them. When he'd left her, she'd been studying the guide he'd created with his sire's journal entries.

Just as he'd expected, he didn't find any signs of officers following them into the forest. First, they probably had no idea they were here. And second, even if they did, the port law enforcement usually stopped any search at the border, especially if the search was for some spoiled merchant's missing slave.

Maybe if there was a large prize for whoever found her, then perhaps the officers would take the risk. But as it sat, if Yanus wanted to look out here in the woods, he'd need to send his own team on the search. That wouldn't happen until daylight.

Most people who didn't know the forest well thought of it as a dangerous place filled with deadly beasts. And in the case of Reka 5, Vosthea, or even the jungles around the largest port on New Rhea, they would be right. This forest, however, was relatively safe.

Kajar entered the cave to find Anna scenting of fear and on high alert. Just the scent of her fear made his cheek creases itch to unfold and let his jaws unhinge and his fangs descend. He was hit with an overwhelming need to protect her and kill anything that threatened her. It confused him. He'd never reacted like this to a female before.

There was nothing dangerous in the cave, and she relaxed visibly the moment he stepped in. He hurried over and pulled her into his arms for a hug. It calmed his need to attack an enemy that didn't exist. Her body felt cold, even though she'd put on another layer in the time he was away.

He started a fire quickly. The cave hid the light of the fire from any watching eyes but also had a hole in the roof to let the smoke escape. It was ideal, and when he'd first found the cave years ago, he couldn't believe his luck.

"Thank you for sharing this with me." She handed back his comm as he sat down on the carved log next to her. "Those drawings and notes are an amazing thing to have of your father."

She pulled out a small piece of paper from the front pocket of her luggage. "This is all I have of Jola and Kortas.

He frowned. She wasn't talking about her own parents, but about a couple who had purchased her only a few years ago, a couple from a completely different species: his.

"A paper image. That's rare to have." Most images were stored on comm units.

"When they transferred me to the Dominion ship, they wouldn't let me keep my comm. I don't know who they thought I'd call. I begged for them to save one of the photos on it for me, and one of the officers printed it out." She tilted the photo in the firelight. "He thought it was strange that I would want to keep a photo of my owners."

"It is," Kajar agreed. He wondered why she would value such a thing.

"They were the first people who ever cared about me." She paused as if not sure if she should tell him more.

"You were alone too. Like me." Kajar imagined Anna as a young female, alone on Earth, and he didn't like it. She would be alone no longer.

"Yeah. Kids on Earth who lose their parents get thrown into the foster care system. Some kids get lucky and find good people who actually care about them. I didn't. I wasn't a bad kid, but I still got pushed from house to house, family to family. I never belonged. I always felt like a burden. When I aged out of foster care, they just kicked me out, and I wasn't surprised." She rubbed at her arms as if trying to warm herself.

Kajar pulled her into his lap, and Anna didn't protest. She just sank into the warmth of his body.

"It felt like I was shoved off the edge of a cliff," she said in a tiny voice.

Kajar knew how that felt. He remembered sitting in his newly acquired ship, wondering how the fuck he was going to survive. At least he'd known his parents, and they'd given him as much as they could.

"I floated around a bit and did what I could, barely keeping food in my belly. Found a few girls like me so we could split on a place and have a roof over our heads. Then I got hired by a strip club, which was, surprisingly, a lucky break. I made enough on the weekends to pay the bills and was able to pick up a barista job during the week. I was saving to go to college when the Dominion spaceships came and rounded me up.

"Moving in with Jola and Kortas was like starting over in a new foster home, except those two actually cared about me. I didn't eat hotdogs on a paper plate while the family fed their own kids real food.

"I lived with them for almost three galactic years. That's longer than anywhere else I've been. They didn't give me up. They kept me until their dying breaths."

Anna had curled up in a ball in his arms as she talked. Kajar nuzzled the top of her head, wishing he knew the words to convince her she was no longer alone.

❈ ❈ ❈

Anna hadn't meant to offload her entire life story on Kajar, but the moment she'd realized he knew how it was to be completely and utterly alone in the universe, the words came pouring out. She hoped it wasn't too much too soon, then decided if Kajar chose to "liberate" her, then he'd have to deal with all parts of her, including her past.

He didn't seem to scare away easily, though, and by the time she finished, she found herself in his lap. Anna leaned against his wide, warm chest and closed her eyes. The fire in front of them chased away the damp in the cave, and the closeness and warmth made her sleepy.

It was his stomach rumbling that interrupted their cozy moment. Anna had almost dozed off in his arms.

Kajar reached over to his pack and brought out two nutrition bars. Anna refused the food, knowing how they tasted. She wasn't hungry enough to eat the bland, cardboardy thing. They'd fed her similar bars on the Dominion ship. She was still full from the delicious wrap from earlier, and it would tide her over to morning.

Kajar inhaled his food, barely chewing it. He'd eaten most of the wrap at the hotel, too. It must take a lot of food to keep those muscles nourished. He washed it down with a few gulps of water. She took a sip as well, glad to have something clean and fresh.

She yawned. It had been an eventful day. While the trek had been easier than she'd first expected, it was still more walking than she'd done in a long time. She kept herself fit but preferred lifting weights in Kortas' personal gym over walking or running. She hated running and would rather do something fun like rock climbing than go for a run.

Kortas had owned a state-of-the-art high-tech rock wall too, one that created handholds and challenges specific to the climber. She missed that a lot.

Kajar was probably right when he'd pinned her as a princess. Over the past few years, she'd gotten used to the good life. Sure, she'd cooked and cleaned for the couple, but they'd also spoiled her like the child they'd never had.

She yawned again, and Kajar stirred. They'd been sitting together, her on his lap, in front of the fire, just cuddling since she'd opened up about her life. It was nice.

"We should set up for bed. I'll let the fire burn for a while to dry out the cave before I bank it for the night."

Anna stood from his lap reluctantly, and Kajar pulled a small bed roll from his bag.

"Wow! You had that in there too? You rented a room at the hotel but came prepared to camp in the woods."

"I always carry my emergency pack with me." He unrolled the sleeping mat a few feet from the fire. "It has everything I need if I have to disappear in the wild for a few days. New Rhea wilderness is easy, so the basics are enough."

"So it's like a bugout bag that you bring everywhere. Isn't that a lot to lug around?"

"The sleeping mat and the blade are the hardest to bring around. Everything else doesn't take up much space: my flask, some nutrition bars, a small medical unit, some cord, and the lantern.

Now that she thought about it, his bag wasn't that large and didn't look out of place while at the port. If anything, it looked like he was heading to the gym, believable too with his muscles. He'd returned to the cave carrying a load of dry wood strapped together with the synthetic cord and the flask tucked into his waistband.

The screeching sound she'd heard earlier sounded again.

"What's that?"

"The mating call of a small animal." He brought out his comm again, scrolled through the drawings, and brought up one of a tiny shrew-like thing. "There must be one in heat in the area. I heard it earlier too."

"There was a clicking sound I heard before as well. What was that?"

"The one that went *tick tick tick*," he mimicked the noise.

"Yeah, that one."

"It's this bird here."

Her translator gave her "avian creature," but she understood it as "bird."

He showed her the image of a strange-looking bird-like creature. "It hunts by locating prey in the dark by clicking."

Anna laughed silently at herself. She'd been terrified of those two tiny things. She'd been such a wimp! All the scary sounds of the forest seemed a lot less menacing now. And not just because she knew what they were, but because Kajar was here.

"Do you camp out a lot?" She leaned against him, resting her head on his shoulder.

"I have a lot of different hideouts on many of the outer planets. Close to the ports but well-hidden. My ship is small, so I don't need clearance to dock at a port. Sometimes I land in the forests unseen."

"You don't like staying in one place, do you?"

"Hate it. I have a hideout on Vosthea next to a waterfall. It's beautiful."

"Will you take me one day?"

He turned to her, serious, and cupped her face in his palms. "I'll take you anywhere you want to go."

His green eyes almost glowed in the fire light, and Anna couldn't look away. She licked her suddenly dry lips, and his eyes followed the movement as if mesmerized.

Anna almost thought they would kiss again, but instead, he released her and got up abruptly.

"You can take my sleeping mat tonight." He picked up the thin nylon-like sheet rolled into the center of the mat, opened it up, and wrapped it around her shoulders. It was light but surprisingly toasty.

"I shouldn't take your spot. Couldn't we both fit on there?" She stood and walked next to him. "The roll is narrow, but if we squish, maybe we'll both fit.

I don't mind sleeping with you."

Kajar cleared his throat awkwardly. "I don't think sharing the mat would be a good idea tonight." He took her hand and pressed to the hardness straining at the front of his pants. "I've decided you deserve better than the floor of a damp cave. When I take you, Anna, it will be in a soft bed on silky sheets."

CHAPTER 6

Kajar clenched his jaw and fisted his hands at his sides as he watched Anna's hips sway in front of him. Despite the cool of last night, this morning was hot and humid. And while she wore the same long, wide-legged pants on the bottom as she did yesterday, she wore nothing but a simple scrap of fabric over her breasts. The shadows of her nipples showed through, and she might as well not have worn anything on top at all.

"I have shorts in here, but I'm not sure I want to have my legs bare for this walk," had been her explanation. Then she'd held up the universe's smallest pair of shorts. They were like a belt with a crotch covering.

Kajar had imagined her in them the entire walk to the water's edge.

She'd insisted on coming to the river with him to refill the flask. She'd had a water bottle in her luggage that he hadn't known about last night, or else he would have filled that too.

He'd warned her not to drink the water from the still pools in the area. The fast-flowing river was clean, but the pools scattered around the area were teeming with parasites. They weren't deadly, particularly not for those with medical units that could detect and eradicate them, but it was still best to avoid them if possible.

"There is one dangerous animal living in this river." Kajar pointed to the deepest area. "The gargapod is a giant-limbed fish that ambushes prey by hiding under the water surface. Sometimes they lunge at animals that come to the water's edge. See that little bump coming out of the water?"

"Yeah, I see it. A limbed fish? So he's like an alligator? I saw a drawing of something that looked like one on your comm, except it had many rows of teeth and a fish tail. The feet were like flippers."

"My translator cannot find this word *alligator*."

"Never mind. How do we make sure he doesn't lunge at us?"

Kajar led her to the calmest spot, an area with many thin, light-green fronds waving in the current.

"These plants not only slow the current, but they also form a thick barrier that prevents the gargapod from getting through without getting tangled. Within the safety of the fronds, we can even bathe."

And there his brain went again, thinking of Anna

naked in the water. He really had to stop. He had to keep his wits about him to keep her safe, and he couldn't do that when every other thought was of her naked in his arms.

She bent by the river and dipped her bottle into the clear, clean water. "Do you think it's safe to bathe? Right now, I mean. We are alone, right? And there isn't anything else dangerous, is there?"

Kajar's mouth went dry, and for a moment, he just stared back at her.

"What?" She looked around at the greenery. "Are there dangerous plants here?"

Kajar swallowed. "No, no dangerous plants here. It is safe to bathe now. If you want."

"Really? That's great! I'm so hot and sweaty." She reached for his belt and unhooked the flask from his waistband, saying, "We might want to fill your flask first."

"Yes. That is best." He'd almost thought she was going to undo his belt. Kajar had to get a hold of himself.

It hadn't helped that in the middle of the night, she'd woken up gasping, and he'd gone to her side. She'd clung onto him and asked him to stay with her, and he had. He'd spent the entire night with her perfect ass pressed back against his front.

Anna'd called it "spooning" and claimed it made her feel safer. Kajar called it torture.

* * *

Anna sent Kajar her sexiest grin as she opened Kajar's flask. Then, making sure he was still watching her, she bent to fill the flask, sticking her ass in the air.

Kajar stifled a groan, and she did a little happy dance in her head. It was working.

Anna teased him on purpose, and she regretted not wearing her short shorts today. The path to the river was much tamer than the path from the wall. Shorts would've helped break his resolve.

She cursed the fact that he was too damned noble to be a space pirate. It was sweet that he wanted to wait for a proper bed and all, but she didn't need that, damn it! She needed him.

It wasn't just because she wanted to secure his interest, so he'd stick with her—she didn't want to be back on the auction block ever again—but because he made her feel things she'd never felt before.

Sleeping with that merchant would've been a chore, something to endure so that she had a roof over her head and food in her belly. But sleeping with Kajar? She couldn't wait. She didn't *want* to wait. She'd wanted a piece of him yesterday.

Anna was attracted to his perfect body, sure. But it was the capable way he held himself, his knowledge of how to survive on his own, that really turned her on. She wanted that in her partner. She also wanted to learn from him and to be just as capable.

Kajar had been on his own, fending for himself for a long time. Anna understood how lonely that could be. He might not even realize it himself. Anna hadn't, not for a long time. She'd mistaken it for anger and disappointment at the never-ending rotation of people in her life. Maybe it had been both.

She handed Kajar his flask back. Then, without skipping a beat, she pulled the tube top over her head and threw it at him with a grin. She stepped out of her silky, wide-legged pants next. Those also got thrown into Kajar's arms. He stood there motionless, slack-jawed, his attention focused solely on her.

"I wish I had a pair of sandals instead, so I could wade right in. I'm not sure about taking my shoes off and stepping into the river."

He swallowed hard before replying. "This area should be safe to go barefoot. These plants usually only grow in sandy regions of the riverbed."

"Perfect!" She kicked off her shoes. Talleans did not wear socks because of their claws, so Anna had gotten used to not wearing them. She stepped into the river, completely naked.

The water was cool and refreshing, a welcome reprieve from the hot, humid air of the forest. When she turned back to look, Kajar had folded her clothes and left them on a rock.

The water was hip-deep here, and she sank in to duck her head under the water. Aside from keeping the larger predators from entering, the many grass-like fronds also filtered the water entering the area without cutting the river's flow and causing the water to go stagnant. The water here was clear, almost crystalline.

She stood again and let the water sheet down her body. It felt good to rinse away the sweat that had accumulated in her hair all morning.

"Come on in, the water is fine! I can't wash my own back, and I don't think I trust the gargapod to do it."

He growled, a look of need and arousal changing his features. His tank top came off first, joining her clothes on the rock, and then the pants. He was already half-hard when he stalked toward her looking every bit the top predator he was.

Anna gulped. He was big everywhere, and even only half-erect, he was impressive. She sure hoped she hadn't bitten off more than she could chew. He prowled toward her, and she backed into the deeper water, excitement growing.

After a few steps, a tangle of fronds stopped her. The mass of fronds formed a perfect little pool and even prevented her from going too far into the river where predators awaited.

She found herself face to face with the most beautifully sculpted chest in the universe, his skin pulled taut over the muscles like soft but tough leather. She had her own predator to contend with. Large hands, rough from work, reached for her hips and pulled her close.

"You've been teasing me all morning, little treasure." Kajar's hands moved, exploring her curves.

"I'm waiting to be ravished, pirate." She tittered at their silly words.

"I've gone through a lot of effort to acquire you. I can't provide you with grand halls and gilded rooms. I can't dress you head to toe in jewels, but I owe it to you to at least provide a soft bed. You deserve more than this." He looked around the forest.

Grand halls, gilded rooms, and jewels? Was Kajar still comparing himself to the merchant who had won the bid? He shouldn't. Just one day with him had changed her mind. She'd left the auction house with the best possible candidate.

"What's wrong with this? We are free and surrounded by nature." She tiptoed to wrap her arms around his neck. "I don't want or need those things, Kajar. I just want you."

CHAPTER 7

So much for Kajar's promise to himself last night. The second Anna's words reached his ears, he was ready to break every promise just to have a taste of her.

With his hands on her rounded buttocks, he lifted her up onto his body, and she instinctively wrapped her lithe legs around his hips. He nuzzled her neck as he carried her to an area where the fronds were especially thick, somewhere far enough from the gargapod that their splashing wouldn't encourage it to try charging through the weeds.

The fronds were so tightly enmeshed here they made a cradle when he laid her upper body down upon it. It kept her at hip level, perfect for him to explore. He bent over her body, kissing every part of it he could reach.

Little fingers entangled in his hair and pulled him up to her face. She kissed his lips the way humans did, and he returned it, claiming her sweet little mouth with his. He darted a tongue into her warmth, and she moaned decadently against him. He enjoyed this claiming of the mouth, this alien tradition.

As he showed Anna what he planned to do soon with her other lips, he trailed a hand down her body, mapping every one of her curves. Her body was small but well-built, and while she would never come close to the bulk of muscles he had, she was no weakling. She was perfect.

He parted her lower lips with his fingers, eager to get to the cream inside. She moaned, and Kajar swallowed the sound with his mouth. Her fingers tightened in his hair as he explored. He found her little nub and rubbed it, watching for her reaction. She rewarded him with a small hiss and an arch of her body.

"Perfect," he groaned. "So perfect."

Leaving her mouth to trail kisses down her body, he made his way to her center, one hand still on her breast to hold her to the floating fronds. With the other hand, he traced her seam with two fingertips before pushing in.

Her lust drowned him in the most seductive perfume, and he longed to taste the source of her honeyed pleasure. Encouraged by her quickened breathing, he covered her mound with his mouth, glad the mat of greenery held her just out of the water. He licked and swirled his tongue over her clit.

Anna cried out, and her channel tightened, the sound clear in the New Rhean forest. Too clear. Kajar reached up with the hand fondling her breast to cover her mouth. When he'd checked the perimeter alarms earlier, he hadn't seen anyone coming from the port, but he didn't want her to give away their location with her cries.

This was a complication he hadn't thought of just a moment earlier. He'd have to muffle her sounds when he fucked her.

Focusing his attention back on her, he suckled hard at her clit and thrust his fingers into her depths. She moaned against his hand, trying hard to keep quiet. Anna had caught on to the need to be quiet as well.

Her eyes were closed now in pleasure, and she panted into his hand. A few more thrusts had her squirming on the bed of buoyant greenery. She screamed into his palm as her channel clenched wildly around his fingers.

He pulled her up from the floating bed.

"Wrap around me, my little treasure," he urged.

She did so, clutching him to her body with ardent need. She burrowed her face into his neck, nuzzling him as a Tallean lover would.

"You need to hold your scream, or else the whole forest will hear you. Can you do that?"

She whimpered. "I don't know. I don't have good vocal control."

Kajar had a solution. "Kiss me," he growled. He pulled her mouth to his, feeding on her lust.

Anna was light in the water, giving him plenty of room to guide the head of his throbbing cock to her entrance. With his hands on her ass guiding them together, Kajar swallowed her cries as he pushed in. Only a small yelp escaped, not enough to give away their whereabouts.

Kajar's eyes rolled up as her creamy cunt enveloped his cock. It was the best feeling in the universe, and he knew that this one time would never be enough. He would crave her every day for the rest of his life.

He kept his mouth on hers as he guided her up and down his cock, his fingers gripping her hips so hard, he was sure they'd leave marks. Anna held him just as tightly, her dull nails digging half-moons into his shoulders.

He shifted their position and found a better angle to thrust in. She moaned and whimpered into the crook of his neck as if trying hard not to scream. He increased his rhythm, and a small sob escaped her lips.

He paused and tilted her head to look into her half-closed eyes. "Are you okay?"

"Yes," she answered between sobs.

"You are crying."

"It's a good cry." She wiggled her hips. "Please, don't stop."

❋ ❋ ❋

Anna couldn't stop her ragged sobbing or the tears that squeezed out of her eyes. What had started as a small sob now took over her entire body. She tried so hard not to scream, but the sensations were so intense they needed a way out. So instead of crying out into the forest, she cried instead into his neck and shoulder, her body shaking with each wracking sob.

She clung to him like he was the only thing in the universe that could save her. There was nothing else in these woods, no, this entire planet, except for them. She inhaled the masculine scent of him, so musky and perfect. She wanted to get lost in it.

His thick cock hit something inside her that ratcheted up the sensations. Her body wound tighter and tighter, like a spring begging to be released. The shaking started in her belly and worked its way to her fingers and toes. And when there was no part of her body that wasn't shaking from the effort to hold herself together, she exploded.

Unable to stop this time, she bit down onto his shoulder and screamed, hoping it would muffle the sound enough. Her body trembled as the euphoria passed over her, turning every bone to jelly, the pleasure so strong all she could see were stars.

He thrust hard a few more times, the rhythm wild and uncontrolled. He snarled as he came, the sound fitting in with the wilderness. His body shook above hers.

They stayed together, both panting in rhythm to the sounds of the forest.

He broke the silence first. "Stay with me," he whispered into her wet hair. "Stay with me always."

She looked up at his gorgeous green eyes and saw the sincerity there. Her heart melted as she realized he'd meant the words. All her life, she'd been passed from place to place, never given a choice. But this, this was her choice. And it was everything she'd hoped for.

"Yes. Always."

He swung her sideways so that he held her in a bridal carry. "You're all dirty again." He smirked. "You're my dirty little treasure."

"Then what are you waiting for? Clean me." She wiggled in his arms with a small chuckle.

He did, washing her from head to toe. He spent extra time washing and detangling her hair. Then he laid out their thin blanket on the bank for them to dry off in the afternoon sun.

Anna relaxed on the blanket and looked up at the few drifting clouds in the sky. "Hey! This planet has two suns! I didn't even notice yesterday. There's the main sun and a smaller one off to the side."

Kajar stretched out next to her, every muscle on display. "I forget that you are new to the outer planets. The two stars take turns warming and lighting the planet. New Rhea doesn't have winter anywhere on its surface. That's why many of the animals are cold-blooded; there's no need to thermally regulate."

"Even the mammal-like creatures in the drawings?"

"Yes, even those. They never evolved to make their own heat; it's not needed here. The nights are the only time it gets cold, but the temperature swing doesn't last long and morning always brings the heat.

It had been chilly last night but bearable. The blanket had been helpful, but she could have survived without it in a pinch.

"It must be nice to be perpetually in summer." Then she wrinkled her nose. "Or horrible, if it's this humid all the time."

"There are seasons, but no winter. There are wet and dry seasons instead, with periods of longer or shorter days."

"And what season are we in now?"

"On this part of the planet, we are transitioning out of the longer wet days, I believe."

That explained the constant dampness in the air. Despite the sun drying them off, she still felt slightly moist. And her hair refused to dry completely.

"Let's go check my traps to see if we caught any dinner."

As Kajar turned, she saw it, her tooth marks on his shoulder. "Oh no! I bit you."

He looked down at the injury and shrugged. "I heal fast. And I don't mind your love bites." He smirked and added, "You've been snapping those teeth at me since the auction house. It's about time you used them."

She wrinkled her nose at him, and he laughed. "Now, the traps."

"Can you show me how to set one up?" If she was going to stay with him, she wanted to be helpful. The first step to that was to learn how to survive. She knew she could depend on him. But she wanted him to be able to depend on her too.

"Of course." He tossed Anna her clothes, and they dressed.

Then she followed him up the river toward his traps. When he'd mentioned traps, she'd thought he meant on land. Instead, he showed her a series of woven nets in the water.

He kept the nets hidden next to the river when not in use. There were no reasons to lug them around with him. He had gear on every planet, cached near his hideouts. It made sense, and it explained why he could travel into the wilderness with so little. He was always prepared, choosing to keep his gear where it was needed so he could travel light.

"One time, I got to the woods near Reka 5 to find most of my stash missing," he said as he pulled the first net out of the water. This one was empty. "The guards from the settlement used the same cave as a hunting cave. Luckily, I'm never in the wilderness there because I'm on the run. I wouldn't borrow anything I didn't absolutely have to from Reka 5. They are good people."

He pulled out the next net, and this one had two good-size fish caught in it. Except they didn't look like normal Earth fish; these creatures looked downright prehistoric. Anna frowned, recognizing them from the drawings on Kajar's comm. They didn't look too appetizing, but she kept that to herself.

"Reka 5—you've mentioned them several times, and every time, I keep thinking it sounds familiar."

"It should, to a slave. Or a former slave. They take in runaways and give them citizenship status as long as they contribute to the colony."

That was where she'd heard of it before. Nolia had told her about it. Nolia was a Tallean slave who'd helped Anna learn her chores when she'd first arrived at Jola's; she'd belonged to a neighbor. Nolia had been taken from her family to make up for a gambling debt when she was still young.

She'd confessed to Anna that she planned on escaping to Reka 5 days before she went missing. Her owners had pounded on the door in a panic early that morning, yelling for Jola to check for Anna. Jola had been so relieved to find Anna still in bed, she'd cried.

Anna had later learned that the way to the freedom of the outer planets was treacherous; many bad males tricked young slaves and trapped them on their ships instead. Many slaves found themselves in worse situations, and some were returned to their owners as corpses. Only those truly desperate and willing to risk dying for the freedom were willing to chance it.

Had Nolia been that unhappy? Anna wondered if she ever found her way to Reka 5.

"Will you take me one day?" She pulled the next trap, and this one was empty.

"We can go right after we leave New Rhea. You'll like it there." He stopped abruptly, a worried look on his face.

"What's wrong?" She looked around. Had he heard something dangerous?

"It's nothing. Let's head back to the cave."

CHAPTER 8

Kajar stepped over the brambles to get to the snares he hadn't checked yesterday with Anna. They'd gotten lucky, and one of the nets had provided dinner. He hadn't wanted to dispatch any cute little animals in front of her. Some of the more civilized Tallean females were squeamish about things like that, especially those from the inner planets. He'd heard humans were the same, and Anna had come from the inner planets.

He'd left her in the cave while he went to check the snares, telling her he didn't want her stepping over the brambles again if it wasn't necessary. It wasn't the same patch of brambles they'd crossed before—this one wasn't as thick—but he didn't mention that. Not wanting to slow him down, she'd agreed to stay in the cave.

One of the snares held one of those cold-blooded mammals they'd discussed yesterday. They were quite tasty if cooked low and slow in the embers of a fire. They would eat well again tonight. He hadn't missed her reaction to the nutrition bars. She'd probably spent the entire time on the Dominion ship eating them.

Kajar also hadn't missed her reaction to Reka 5. He had told her she was free. He didn't own her. Would Anna choose to stay on Reka 5 instead of living a nomadic life with him? There were other humans there. Human males. They could give her stability, a real home in a friendly colony.

Anna would be safe from the Dominion. Most citizens on Reka 5 would fight to the death to avoid being slaves again under Dominion rule. They had fought the Dominion off before and would again.

Kajar rubbed at the tight lump forming in his chest. He couldn't guarantee this if she stayed with him. He would fight to his last breath to keep her safe, though. But he was only one male and couldn't compare to the safety of an entire colony.

Would he be willing to stay on Reka 5 with her and give up his life of wandering? Traveling was all he knew. His early life with his sire and mother had always been on the move. Even after they were gone, it was clear he'd been made from the same space dust. The Stars called to him even if he didn't always believe in them.

Kajar knelt by the river to clean and gut the animal as he let his mind wander, throwing the innards into the water. They were greedily gobbled up by the hungry denizens.

There was always the Mercenary Alliance compound. His parents had been part of the Alliance, visiting the compound every so often to pick up missions to make some credits. The people there knew Kajar, had watched him grow as a youngster every time they visited. His mother's sister lived there still.

He hadn't gone back much after losing his parents, except to find work when times were lean. But there weren't many missions a loner like him could take. Larger crews did better in space.

Some mercenaries chose to leave their mates safe in the compound while they worked. But the idea of leaving Anna alone anywhere held no appeal. It hadn't to his sire either; he'd brought his family everywhere on his little ship.

A family. He'd heard talk on Vosthea about the possibility of Tallean-Human hybrid offspring. He imagined Anna round with his child and rubbed at his chest again.

What was wrong with him? They'd just met yesterday, and he was already thinking of a family. He had been consumed with thoughts of her ever since seeing her on the auction block. Could this be a mating bond?

Kajar froze. A mate. Anna could be his mate. That would explain these strange and foreign emotions taking over his head.

His comm buzzed on his belt. He checked it and a cold dread sunk into his chest. Something had triggered the sensor at the wall. Wild animals wouldn't trigger that one; only the door opening would. Yanus had sent his males out to look for Anna after all.

Kajar had left Anna with his large bag and sleeping mat. Even if Anna left the cave before they found it, they would find the equipment and know they were here. If Anna took his bag and mat with her, they would slow her down and make her easier to spot.

Yanus might not have seen them escape or even known that they were in the wilderness, but he'd sent males to check, just in case. He'd paid a lot for Anna, and Kajar doubted Yanus would see a single credit back after they gave him the key to her room. It had been Yanus who had "lost" the key.

Kajar had to get back to her now. He'd never had a partner before, and he wasn't going to let them take his first and only.

* * *

Anna rolled up their sleeping mat and pushed all their gear toward the back of the cave. Then she piled as many leaves and branches as she could drag in over their supplies to hide them.

The voices still sounded far away, but it was clear as day that they were looking for her. They weren't happy about it either, and one of the males had roared and cursed loudly at the brambles latched around his legs. That had been what alerted Anna of the approaching pair.

She needed to get out of the cave. If they found her here, there would be nowhere for her to run and hide. Now that the idea of freedom was possible, she never wanted to be a slave again. Out in the wilderness, she had a chance.

She tied the openings of her pant legs with two strips she'd ripped off the hem of a tank top so they wouldn't impede her travels. She should have thought of this earlier, but hey, necessity was the mother of invention.

She poked her head out to survey her exit, then darted out of the cave and toward the river. Kajar had mentioned he placed his traps close to water to catch any small animals going in for a drink. It was the best chance for her to meet up with him.

She only took a few steps before she doubled back, realizing the males would scent her and Kajar if they found the cave. She headed toward the patch of stinky weeds, hoping she got there undetected before her hunters did.

Keeping low to the ground, she gathered as many of the horrible red flowers as she could. The stench made her want to hurl, but she held her breath as she rubbed the disgusting smell all over her clothes. That should hide her scent well. Kajar had said they didn't only smell bad, they messed up his sense of smell as well.

Then she gathered more; she planned on rubbing them onto the walls of the cave and leaving the crushed up flowers everywhere near the opening. But as she made her way back to the cave, voices stopped her.

"I can't believe that spoiled prick is making us look for her out here. Even if she did make it out, what are the chances she's still alive?"

"I heard there are killer beasts in these woods. She'd be a tasty treat."

The males made a lot of noise as they trudged through the forest. They hadn't planned on using stealth to find her. Every living thing in the forest heard them coming a mile away.

There were only two of them, but two were enough if they found her without Kajar's protection.

"Hey, look over there, a cave. Let's check it out."

"How do we know some wild animal doesn't live there?"

"I don't think wild animals could cut a hole in the brush like that to get to their home."

Shit! So much for covering up their scents. The moment they stepped into that cave, they would know she and Kajar were here.

Anna knew it was a risk, but she needed to cover up the trail leading to the carrion plants. While the two males checked out the cave, she ran out to the path, crushed up the flowers in her hands, tried not to gag, and scattered them everywhere. Then she ran back into the brush, ducking behind a bush.

Now, when they tried to track her, they would hopefully follow the aborted path to the river.

"I can't believe Yanus was right. She's out here. Whoever stole her must be an idiot." The male spat at the entrance to the cave. His pant leg was mangled, cut haphazardly with a knife to his calf. The skin underneath had cuts and scratches from the brambles.

"We got a scent now and tracks too." The other male pointed to the ground. "We can follow them, get the female back, and get that bonus."

They didn't follow her abandoned trail from earlier but instead went for the deeper one they'd left yesterday from their trip down to the river.

Anna had two choices: keep her eyes on her enemy, or look for Kajar. But what if Kajar was in their path? Two against one didn't seem good odds, especially since these two males had blasters strapped to their belts.

She couldn't lose sight of them; it was too dangerous. If they bumped into Kajar and things looked bad, she would come out of hiding to distract them. But until then, she planned on following them, hiding in the dense greenery. She didn't want them to sneak up on her; right now, she had the upper hand.

She followed them, making as little noise as possible, to the river's edge. They walked up and down the river bank where she and Kajar had spent time yesterday.

"Looks like we are going across. Their trail ends here."

"The river looks calm." The male tucked the knife he had in his hands into the side of his boot. "Just focus on the bonus."

"It better be good." Then he waded into the water, away from the protective fronds, and the other male followed him in.

They made it about a quarter of the way across the river before there was a disturbance in the water. Then the first male screamed, flailing violently. Flashes of rough, bumpy scales showed at the surface as red streamed into the river.

"What the fuck is that?"

The flailing male screamed a nonsensical answer as his buddy pulled him out of the river. Attached to his thigh was a prehistoric-looking beast as long as Anna was tall. It looked exactly as it had in the drawing, a mix between a primeval fish and a gator.

The male not having his leg ripped to shreds shot the thing with his blaster. In his haste, he'd left the device on stun, but it was enough to get the creature to release the other male's leg. He kicked the creature with his clawed foot, pushing it toward the water.

The other male's leg didn't look good.

The gargapod shook itself off and, deciding the meal wasn't worth it, pushed itself up on its modified fins and lumbered back into the river.

If it weren't for the sheer size of these Tallean males, the gargapod would've had a great lunch.

"Fuck! This! Shit!" the male with the injured leg swore, as he ripped a piece of his top and wrapped it around his wounds. "I'm going back. The female is dead if she went into that water. If you want that bonus, it's yours if you find her. Take my share. I'm heading back. I need a medical device now."

"Fuck the bonus. They're probably dead. It's not like Yanus will miss her. He'll just buy a new one." Then he helped his friend to stand, and the two hobbled back the way they came.

Anna stayed there, unmoving, until they were out of sight. She doubted she'd see them again.

It wasn't until she pushed herself up to standing that she saw it: the dino-bird from the drawings. Except it wasn't the size of a flamingo as she'd thought, it was the size of a grizzly bear. And it was looking right at her.

CHAPTER 9

Kajar ducked into the foliage as the two males limped past, one favoring a leg that was already bleeding right through the makeshift bandage. He'd heard the screaming coming from the river moments after returning to the cave to find it abandoned and smelling of strange males.

His first thought had been anger that these strange males had his Anna. But all signs showed the males had left alone, and there had been no skirmish. The masculine screaming had reassured him that his Anna was safe.

These must be the two males Yanus had sent to find his missing merchandise. It seemed they'd found something with a little more teeth instead. From their conversation, Kajar knew they wouldn't be back; they were convinced Anna had met her demise in the wilderness and planned on telling their boss the same.

Now all he had to do was find his female. From the scent of the carrion plant and the crushed flowers strewn onto the trail in front of the cave, he knew what to follow. Chemicals in the carrion plants messed up his sense of smell. He couldn't follow her trail, but it was pungent enough that he could follow the stench itself now that he knew what to look for.

His female was quick thinking to use the carrion plant to hide her scent. She'd also hidden their equipment and packs well behind a pile of branches and leaves. She'd stayed just out of sight in the thick brush and had followed the two males down to the river. She must still be there, possibly looking for him.

Kajar hurried toward the water.

What he saw sent chills down his spine. Anna had squeezed herself into the hollow of a tree next to the river and was defending herself from the deadly beak of a scavenger bird with nothing more than a stick. She'd been smart to hide in the tree, as it protected her sides and flank. That little branch was not enough to stop the bird, though, especially if she smelled of carrion.

The bird usually didn't hunt living things. It served as the eco system's all-purpose garbage disposal, feasting off the dead and decaying. It knew the carrion plants were not food, recognizing the red flowers as a decoy. But with Anna scenting of the carrion flower and the scent of the male's blood all over the riverbank, this bird was confused.

It towered over Anna and shrieked before driving its head forward and pecking with its deadly beak.

Kajar only had a moment's notice before the bloodlust consumed him. Adrenaline pumped through his veins, imbuing him with enhanced reflexes. He changed, letting his cheek creases unfold and his jaw unhinge. Then his fangs lengthened, extending from their half-retracted resting position.

This larger, more deadly bite, combined with the eight sharp claws on his feet and the altered, quickened senses of bloodlust, made Kajar a deadly fighter. Some more civilized folks preferred to ignore this adaptation from their past—a past of hunting and fighting—but Kajar never claimed he was civilized. He felt at home in the wilds.

Kajar roared, the sound echoing in the forest. Some creatures ran and hid in their burrows, while others fled from the primal sound.

Finally noticing another predator, the scavenger bird screeched and postured, trying to scare away the competition. It wouldn't work; Anna was his and his alone.

Kajar tapped the long claws of his feet on the ground as a warning, but the bird ignored it. It wasn't the smartest of creatures. Most heard the threat in the clicking of a Tallean's claws, but this bird heard it as a challenge instead, eager to keep the foul-smelling morsel to itself.

It turned to face him, spreading its wings in a form of intimidation. While its blunt, heavy wings no longer afforded it flight, they were formidable weapons. One hit from those appendages broke bones and knocked its enemy out. It screeched again and scratched at the ground the way it did before it charged.

This bird was messing with the wrong Tallean.

Kajar didn't give the creature time to charge; he attacked, running in with a swift jumping kick to the creature's neck. He ripped out two large clawfulls of quill-like feathers. The protofeathers were not useful for flight or temperature regulation; instead, their sole purpose was defense.

The creature screamed, angry about being involuntarily plucked. If it knew what was good for it, it would have run because Kajar planned to do much more than pluck it if it insisted on attacking his female. But the creature launched an attack, leaping at Kajar with its own clawed feet extended. Kajar danced out of the way.

He tackled the bird from the side, knocking it into the trunk of a tree with a thud.

Out of the corner of his eyes, Kajar saw Anna's tiny form crawl out of the tree's hollow and up into the branches. She was strong and was able to lift herself onto the branch above. Just a little higher, and the deadly creature would no longer be able to reach her.

Kajar wasn't the only one to notice the movement. The creature charged toward the tree and leaped, trying to reach its escaping prey with its beak. That beak was designed to tear into carcasses and crush bones to get at the fatty marrow inside. Kajar couldn't let it get a hold of Anna. He dove for the thing's thick legs, knocking its feet from under it. It missed Anna by a hair's width. It landed on the forest floor and flailed its wings, trying to right itself.

Taking advantage of the creature's position, Kajar gripped it by its ankles and swung, putting his entire weight into the movement. It was heavy, outweighing him by far, but he managed to swing it into the water.

The gargapod, not believing its good luck, charged for the rare treat. It wasn't often it had the opportunity to sink its teeth into prey that size. Loud squawking and violent splashing ensued before the scavenger bird climbed out the opposite bank, a chunk missing from its rump.

Having had enough of this encounter, it turned tail and fled.

Instincts told Kajar to chase, but something else called to him. He turned to the little human female perched precariously on a branch and headed toward his prize.

✷ ✷ ✷

Anna had never seen a Tallean go into bloodlust before, but she'd heard about the ability many times. It wasn't supposed to be done in polite company by civilized males. She'd been told it was a barbaric thing, reserved for uncouth mercenaries, fighters in a ring, and lawless pirates.

She didn't care because this barbarian of a space pirate had just saved her life.

Kajar prowled toward her, his teeth still extended. He growled with every breath and looked terrifying, but something told her he would never hurt her. This was Kajar. He was her protector.

She looked down at the ground below. She'd climbed up out of desperation but had no idea how to get down; a drop from this height could be dangerous. The solution presented itself as Kajar got close, extending his strong muscular arms.

She pushed off the branch and into his embrace, trusting him to catch her. He would never drop her.

"You came for me," she whispered into the side of his neck.

He answered with a low growl and started toward their cave.

Anna had an idea what was coming. Even on the inner planets, Tallean males fought, though rarely in bloodlust. And after each fight, the males were often horny, as were the females who stayed to watch the violence. Despite their mask of civility, Talleans were unable to completely suppress their instincts. They loved violence, and they loved sex. And the one often led to the other.

Anna didn't care about civility. She was just glad to be in his arms, and if he needed her right now to slake his violence-induced lust, she was happy to oblige.

Her legs wrapped instinctively around his hips as he carried her to safety. She nuzzled his neck, using the Tallean display of affection. He was slightly sweaty from the heat and his recent exertion, and it smelled good: earthy, woodsy, and pure maleness. She licked his skin and hummed happily.

He growled and palmed her ass, pulling them together. Something hard and insistent bumped against her with each step, and she moved her hips to rub against it.

He ducked under the vines and foliage at the opening of their cave and entered their temporary home. He didn't put her down. Instead, with one hand supporting her, he brushed aside the branches hiding their gear and wrestled the mat onto the ground.

She quickly found herself on her back on the mat with most of her clothes ripped off her body. He was above her in an instant, equally naked. His fangs, jaws, and cheeks had returned to normal, but there was still a feral look in his eyes.

"You are safe," he murmured into her neck between kisses and licks. "I need you."

"I'm yours." She wrapped her legs around his hips, pressing her pussy against the length of him, and rocked her hips. It felt good, and seeing him like this turned her on. He wanted her so much it looked like he would die without her. It made her wet and ready.

He snarled, sounding barely in control. "I need to go slow. You are so small."

"Forget slow. I want you now." She was already slick with need and had no more patience for foreplay. She rocked her hips again, sliding her slit along his shaft.

That did it. He lined them up and pushed in.

She cried out, then covered her mouth, panting and worried. "The two males. What if they aren't gone yet."

"They left and won't be back. We are safe. Scream all you like." He pulled out slightly and thrust back in, penetrating a few inches deeper.

She cried out again at the intense sensation. It felt as if he'd split her in half in the best way possible.

A few more thrusts and he was fully seated. He gave her a few moments to get used to him before he moved.

"Yes!" she hissed.

Anna clung to him and threw her head back, panting heavily. Kajar was merciless as he thrust into her again and again, the force of it moving the entire mat beneath them. It was the most amazing thing she'd ever felt, and she surrendered to him as his cock grew even larger and harder inside her. She panted in rhythm to his movements as her climax threatened.

A loud, desperate moan tore from her throat as her body wound tighter and tighter. Kajar snarled, and the primal sound threw her over the edge. She shook from head to toe as the climax stole her senses.

Kajar continued thrusting into her as she peaked, threatening to keep her there for an eternity until there was nothing left of her but a quivering mass. It was too much; she screamed again as she crested a second time, barely moments after the first. Then Kajar joined her with a vicious snarl and pulled her tight to his body as he bathed her insides with his hot seed.

He rolled them so she lay on top of him. Tired from everything that had happened already, even though the day was far from over, Anna closed her eyes and rested her cheek on his chest. In the safety of his arms and with his heartbeat as her lullaby, she slept.

CHAPTER 10

Kajar grinned as he watched Anna skip through the market stalls of Reka 5. Yesterday, when they'd first arrived on the colony, she'd been reserved, sticking next to him for safety. She hadn't truly believed humans were equals here and slavery didn't exist. After meeting many escaped slaves, both human and Tallean, she relaxed and started to enjoy herself.

He'd chosen to stay in the colony and rent a room at the inn instead of camping out in the woods. He wanted to show her around and spend some quality time together.

Anna already knew he was comfortable in the wilderness. For the past few light cycles, he'd proven to her that life on his ship was comfortable, even though they'd spent most of the trip to Reka 5 in his bed. He wanted to show her he could navigate his way through the different ports and colonies as well. He wasn't rich, but he could provide for her and keep her safe.

Today, they were at the large market where local vendors and traveling merchants set up booths to peddle their wares. Anna flitted from stall to stall, looking at both the mundane items and the oddities with equal delight. She also looked around the market at the faces of the shoppers as if she were looking for someone.

Was she? Anna *had* asked for him to bring her here. Did she have a friend she hoped made it to the colony? From the inner planets, the voyage to Reka 5 would have been perilous. Not just from the fear of being caught but also knowing who to trust.

Kajar searched for someone as well. Jakkan set up shop for a short period on Reka 5 every planetary orbit to sell Earth-made merchandise. Merchandise Kajar often had a hand in acquiring without passing any credits to the Dominion. The Dominion had taken too much from the planets they'd conquered already.

But Jakkan was nowhere to be seen. He must be late getting to the colony this year. Too bad. Kajar had been excited about looking through his wares with Anna. He wanted to spoil her, show her that he could provide for her as well as any merchant—what better way than with items from Earth?

Even if she didn't miss any of the people from her home planet, there must be other things she missed. He'd heard of a magical food called chalk-a-let that wooed Earth females reliably. He knew it was one of the items Jakkan had trouble keeping in stock.

Living on his ship and off the land meant Kajar saved much of what he earned. His greatest expenses were fuel, repairs, and upgrades for his ship. He did supplement his diet with purchased nutrition bars or ship rations, but it was a small part of his costs since he foraged and hunted often. Some sweet treats wouldn't set him back at all.

"Anna?"

Anna stopped mid-step and turned to the female voice.

"Anna! You made it." A Tallean female flung herself onto Anna and hugged her.

"Nolia!" Anna hugged her back. "I wasn't sure I would find you. Wow! You look good." She pushed herself away to look at her friend.

"I didn't think you wanted to leave Jola and Kortas. You seemed happy there. If I knew you wanted to leave, I would have taken you with me."

Kajar stepped back, feeling like a third wheel at this reunion.

Anna looked down at her hands. "I didn't. Jola and Kortas are," she said, then paused, "They're with the Goddess now."

"I'm sorry."

Anna cleared her throat. "Which reminds me, I haven't heard a bell all day."

Nolia beamed. "We can believe in whatever we want here. Most of us believe in the Stars."

Anna turned to Kajar then and introduced him to Nolia. "She's one of the reasons I wanted to visit Reka 5."

"Visit?" Nolia looked disappointed. "You're not staying?"

Kajar stiffened. He'd been trying not to think of the possibility Anna would choose to stay on Reka 5. He'd told himself that Anna cared for him and felt safer around him, so would prefer to keep his company instead. But if she had a friend here already, that changed things.

Suddenly needing to feel the touch of her skin, he put an arm around Anna possessively.

Nolia narrowed her eyes at his action. "Well then, since you've found me, we should catch up. I'm heading over to the public baths. Join me. We can catch up. Just the two of us."

"I don't have any credits." Anna turned to him with a hopeful look in her eyes.

Nolia sent Kajar a dirty look, and he rubbed the back of his neck awkwardly. Nolia must think he was her owner, especially since Anna didn't have her own credits. She probably thought he made Anna ask him before doing anything.

This was a safe colony. Anna wouldn't be in any danger here. Kajar had told her she was free, and he kept his word. Even if a part of him wanted to hide her away and keep her to himself forever.

"Of course. Use my credit tag." He handed her his

spare, glad that he'd gotten the extra one made years ago. It was the first time he'd needed it. "The baths are close to one of the stores where I need to pick up supplies at anyway."

Worry grew all through the transport ride to the baths as Kajar listened to the two females talk. Nolia made Reka 5 out to be the perfect place to live. A place to start fresh and be her own person. She told Anna there were so many humans here the culture was thoroughly mixed; they even shook hands and gave high fives, whatever those were.

There was so much about her culture he didn't know. He hadn't even thought to ask.

"She'll comm you when we're done." Nolia took Anna by the arm and led her toward the bathhouse.

Kajar resisted the urge to pull Anna into his arms, stuff her back into his ship, and fly off, never to land on this colony again. What if the next time he saw Anna, she insisted on staying on this perfect colony with her friend?

"Wait, I don't have a comm."

Nolia turned back and glared at Kajar, a disgusted look on her face. "You can use mine."

Damn it. He was not making a good impression on her friend at all. That would have been one of the first things he got her so they could contact each other. Unless of course, he expected her to be at his side always, like a servant. That hadn't been it at all. They'd been together the whole time and simply hadn't needed to contact each other. It had slipped his mind.

Kajar stared at the back of Anna's head as she entered the bathhouse. Then she was inside, leaving him alone with his doubt.

Anna struggled to understand her friend's words as she sat in the steamy, fragrant water of the giant main pool.

"I mean it, Anna. The guards here will protect you if you want to leave Kajar. They will ban him from the colony if they have to. You can stay here."

There must be some sort of misunderstanding. Nolia thought she stayed with Kajar because she was afraid to leave. That couldn't be further from the truth.

"You don't have to stay with a thief who stole you from an auction."

"It's not like that at all. I want to stay with him. I like Kajar."

"Are you sure? He didn't even give you a comm. Not even one of those locked ones they give to slaves, the ones with tracking that can only call home. Is it because he never let you leave his side before?"

"It's because I haven't had the need to leave his side yet, and this is the first place he took me. I asked him to bring me here and he did."

Nolia pressed her lips together. "Are you staying out of gratitude? For getting you out of the slave market?"

Anna chose her words carefully. "I am thankful he stole me away, but that's not why I stay with him. Listen, I know you're just worried about me. And I appreciate it, I do. I'm sure Reka 5 is a great place to live. But you know that feeling of finally realizing you belong somewhere? That feeling of finally being home?"

"Yeah." Nolia smiled. "I found that here."

"Well, I found it with Kajar. I know our meeting was unorthodox, but I chose to run off with him into the wilds. And I'm going to choose him again now."

Her friend sighed and sank into the swirling water to her chin. "Okay. I believe you. I got worried because he was acting like he owned you. And you didn't have a comm or your own credit tag and had to ask his permission to do things."

"I haven't exactly had the chance to make my own credits yet. And I didn't feel comfortable volunteering his credits for a girl's day out."

Anna had never gone to a public bath before, though she'd known of them. Slaves weren't allowed inside unless they were serving their owners. She did know it was a common pastime for Talleans. It was a place to relax and socialize. And many found their future mates at the baths.

Nolia took a deep breath of the berry-scented air around them, looking pensive. "Maybe I read his possessiveness wrong. I wonder—" She didn't finish her sentence.

"Don't get cryptic with me. What do you wonder?"

"Has he mentioned anything about a mating bond?"

Mating bond? That was the sign of forever after when two Talleans fell in love. Jola and Kortas had a mating bond, and he'd followed her to the grave. Jola had passed first, and Kortas had followed after even though he'd been healthy just days before. A couple with a mate bond never strayed, and one-sided bonds were considered a curse.

"That's," Anna sputtered, "that's impossible! I'm a human."

Nolia looked at her like she'd just said something really silly. She sighed. "I keep forgetting how much they kept from us on the inner planets. We can absolutely form mating bonds with humans. Look around you."

Anna had noticed the many Tallean-human couples on Reka 5. They were not only common, but they publicly showed affection the way Tallean couples did on the inner planets, which was to say they had no public filter when it came to expressing their love. But she'd thought they were just couples, partnerships of convenience. Were some of these couples true mates?

She peered around the bathhouse. They were in the large communal tub, the size of a swimming pool, and across from them was a Tallean male holding a human female in his arms like a baby. They whispered to each other and occasionally punctuated their sweet nothings with kisses. A little way over, a human man with tattoos on his shoulders held onto a Tallean female with a heart-shaped face, their eyes closed, enjoying the bath.

"It's true, isn't it."

"Sure is. And if his possessiveness doesn't stem from some archaic and oppressive sense of ownership, then maybe he's forming a mating bond. The question is, do you want to be stuck with him for the rest of your life?"

Did she want a mating bond with Kajar? With strong, capable, knowledgeable Kajar, who understood how it felt to struggle with life alone?

"I—I think so. I really care about him. But we don't know for sure it's a mating bond."

"No, we don't." Nolia angled her body to look at Anna seriously. "Anytime you need to get out of your situation for any reason at all, just say the word, and we'll get you. But if it ends up being a mating bond, then I'm happy for you."

"Thank you." Anna leaned over to hug her friend. "But enough about me. Tell me how you made it to Reka 5 and everything that's happened since."

CHAPTER 11

Kajar paced outside the baths with his packages of supplies. He'd tried sitting on the bench, but his doubt and nervousness demanded he move.

Reka 5 was a great place to live, especially for someone like Anna. There were other humans here and other escaped slaves she could relate to. She could become a citizen, get a job, and settle down here. She wouldn't need to follow him around the galaxy, never staying still for any length of time.

She could make a life on Reka 5. She already had a friend here—one who, he reminded himself, already didn't like him. With time, she would make more. She would meet males, maybe humans, maybe Talleans: males who could give her a stable life in an established colony. Males who wouldn't drag her from planet to planet, never able to settle down.

He looked around at the quaint little town the colony had built to be their city center and at the couples and families enjoying their day off. How could his beat-up little ship ever hold a candle to this?

He heard Anna's laughter before he saw her, the sound pulling at his heart as if she owned him. He'd technically stolen her from the auction house, but she'd stolen his heart and held all the cards. She could destroy him in an instant, and there was nothing he could do.

She stepped out of the bathhouse, arm looped around her friend's, and Kajar swore she almost glowed like the Stars themselves. He took a step toward her, and she noticed him. She waved, smiling. As if with a mind of their own, his feet carried him to her until they were face to face.

Anna released her friend and threw her arms around him as he stood there awkwardly, both hands occupied by his packages.

Finally, he got his throat to work. "Did you have fun?"

"Yes, thank you." She took one look at his full arms and hooked her arm into his elbow. She turned back to her friend. "Thanks for everything. I'll call you the moment I get my hands on a comm, I promise."

Nolia looked up at him, at first with scrutiny in her eyes, then her eyes softened. "Bring Anna back to visit often, will you?"

"I will." He didn't mention that there was a chance

Anna would just stay here.

The two said their goodbyes, and Kajar called a transport to take them to the ship. Anna told him all about the baths and her friend's journey to the colony during the transport ride. She was so animated he couldn't help but smile back even though the possibility of losing her still sat heavily on his mind.

What was wrong with him? He'd entertained the possibility that this feeling he had for Anna was a mating bond, and now, he was sure. He'd formed a mating bond with her and now had to choose between his love of traveling and his love of her. He knew which would win in the end.

They entered his ship, and he looked around the familiar place, wondering if he could ever give this up. This was the last thing he had of his parents.

Anna plopped down on the couch, kicked off her shoes, and propped her cute little feet up on the armrest like she owned the place. He committed the image to his memory in case he wouldn't see it again in the future.

No. If he had to give up this ship to be with her, he would. There was no way he would let Anna find someone else on this colony. She was his.

"After we drop the supplies off, are we going to pick up the traveling gear for me?"

Here it was; she was going to tell him the traveling gear wasn't necessary.

Before he could reply, she pulled him down onto

the couch, reached for his face, and tilted it to her. "What's wrong? Why do you look so sad?"

The words stuck in his throat, and he forced them out one by one. "I know you like the colony. We can stay here if you want. I'll stay with you if you'll have me."

She frowned. "Stay? But what about your ship or traveling? I know you always like to be on the move. You can't stay here." She pushed herself upright. "Where's all this coming from?"

Stars! Why was this so hard?

"I can not leave without you. You are my mate, Anna. I'm sure of it. I can not let you find someone else here. I will stay with you."

She wrapped her arms around him, and kissed him soundly on the mouth.

"Who the hell said anything about staying?"

✣ ✣ ✣

Anna hugged Kajar hard, trying to push away the sadness and doubt that oozed out of him.

So, this was what bothered Kajar. He'd been quiet the whole ride home, and it had her worried that he wasn't feeling well. He believed she would want to stay here now that she'd seen everything the colony had to offer.

Reka 5 was beautiful, full of nature, and well-designed. Throw in a friend and the ability to become a citizen and live a good life, and the deal could be very tempting indeed. It was a good option, a smart one. But one that held no appeal to her, especially if staying meant Kajar would need to give up the nomadic life he enjoyed. And staying without him was out of the question.

Then it hit her. Kajar had just told her she was his mate!

"Wait! Say it again."

"I will stay with you?"

"No, back more, the part about me being your mate."

"You are, Anna. You're my mate. That must be the only explanation why I feel this way. It feels like being apart from you could kill me." His brows furrowed, and his fists clenched at his sides. "If you wanted to prevent it from happening, it's too late. It's already done. You are it for me."

Her vision blurred as her eyes filled with happy tears.

Kajar saw the tears and stiffened, a look of defeat in his eyes. "The thought of being my mate upsets you."

"No, no! Kajar. These are happy tears. I am happy to be your mate."

Anna mentally chided herself. Kajar must think humans cried at everything: sadness, anger, good sex, and now happiness too.

"You are?"

Anna nodded, unable to speak. Then she latched onto him and cried. "Ugh! I'm so pathetic. You tell me I'm the one and all I can do is cry on you." She wiped at her eyes. "I'm not interested in staying, Kajar. Maybe one day in the future, if we get sick of traveling, we can make a home here. But not now. Not yet. I want to travel with you." She gestured around the ship. "This is home." She looked at him. "You are home."

"But this colony offers you so much more than I—"

She didn't let him finish.

"Don't be silly. I love you, Kajar. Why would I ever ask you to be unhappy to stay with me? And why would I ever want to be anywhere you are not? And besides, you promised to take me many places. I'm holding you to that. I want to see the galaxy."

He cupped her face in his hands and pulled her in to nuzzle her nose with his. "I'll take you anywhere you want."

"And I'll follow you anywhere you go. And that's not a promise. That's a threat. You'll never get rid of me!" She grinned at him.

"I'd never dare." He picked her up and spun her around. "I love you too. I'm all yours from now until the Stars cease to shine. And you're all mine, little treasure." A twinkle of mischief flashed in his eyes. "Even if you do bite."

Anna growled, imitating him the best she could, and snapped exaggeratedly at him with her teeth. "You betcha I do!"

There, on a little ship, in the outer planets, Anna found the one place in the entire universe she would always feel at home, in the arms of her alien pirate mate.

EPILOGUE

Kajar rolled his eyes and held his tongue as his aunt fussed over Anna.

He'd returned to the Mercenary Alliance compound to pick up a proper mission for the first time since he'd had Anna on board. The compound was tight-knit, and news that he'd returned with a female in tow had traveled fast.

Ecca had come racing in to meet the Earth female her nephew had taken as a mate.

"Your parents would be so proud of you!" Then she turned to Anna. "Look at you! Such a pretty female. You're a tiny thing. Is Kajar feeding you well? And look at that shiny black hair! I kept one of his mother's combs. It would look lovely on you."

Anna sent him a look of utter panic. She had not been prepared to meet family of any type.

"Um, ah," she stuttered awkwardly.

"Oh, I'm sorry, I haven't even introduced myself. I'm Ecca. Kajar's mother was my younger sister. I miss them terribly. And this one here," she gestured to Kajar, scolding, "never comes back to visit. You need to get him to return more often. I told him the Alliance would take care of him, but he's just like his sire, that one. Constantly needs to move around."

Anna cleared her throat. "Nice to meet you. I'm Anna. I'm sure we will be back more often. We're planning on taking some extra missions to build a nest egg."

His aunt turned to him. "There aren't many missions available for those who work alone, but I'll get them to save some for you." Then she frowned. "You aren't thinking about having this poor female wait alone on the ship while you work, are you? She's going to be so bored. Oh, I know! She could stay here, safe with the other mates and children."

His aunt faced him, so she didn't see Anna cringe. Kajar did. Staying at the compound with the other mates, alone without him, was not her idea of fun. Their idea of fun always included each other.

"She's fine with me on the ship."

"Yes, I'm fine. Kajar promised to show me the galaxy."

His aunt sighed. "You are like my sister. Happy to travel with her mate wherever he went. I am happy for both of you. May the Stars look kindly on your mating." She placed her fist on her chest, pinky side out: a sign of respect and well wishes.

They returned the gesture, and she left them as they finished the refueling and restocking of the ship.

"You should have seen your face when she suggested you stay on the compound with the other mates. You looked like you were about to flee."

Anna shuddered. "I couldn't imagine being stuck here talking house with the ladies when you are out there having fun. No way!"

"I used to think I was happy out there on my own, that I didn't need anyone. I realize now how wrong I was."

"Yeah? How so?" She grinned at him, knowing his answer.

"I need you." He caught her by the waist and pulled her close.

"I need you, too." She kissed him on the nose.

Kajar buried his face into the crook of his mate's neck, nuzzling her. It took him scouring the galaxy to find his treasure, and now that he had her, he would never let her go. Not now. Not ever.

THE END

EXCERPT FROM A CLAIM FOR CALIX

Calix fingered the hidden blade through his pant leg, but he doubted he would need it during this simple escorting mission. He leaned against the soft back of his chair. Anyone watching would think he was relaxed, but Cal was on high alert.

It was a simple mission: get the merchant safely to his destination and protect him during the deal. Cal had done this plenty of times. And this time, he even had the help of the establishment the merchant chose to conduct the discussion at.

The Meeting Ground was a neutral zone that companies and crews could rent out to conduct business. The establishment provided refreshments, entertainment, and all the armed guards required should the deal go sour. Other people's business was their business, and they were damn good at it. Most likely,

Cal's services wouldn't be required until they left the establishment for their ships.

A server came by and filled their drinks. Cal accompanied their merchant client with two others from his crew. Vosken was an experienced mercenary and an exceptional fighter, and Grissom was young, fast, and a quick study. Cal often trained with both males and knew they would have his back.

The host, an older male with a distinguished air, appeared by the door, and all parties turned to face him.

"Thank you for choosing the Meeting Ground to be your neutral zone. Here at our prestigious establishment, we believe that the best way to avoid excessive violence is to make sure all other needs are met, and met well. We provide award-winning food and drink, as well as female distractions to help calm frayed nerves during your business transaction."

Three females walked in, heads bowed. Their host brought a rounded human female towards Cal and his group. "You males look like you may need some female flesh."

Cal raised his hand to reject the distraction. He knew what the host was trying to do. The Meeting Ground offered females to distract those they believe may instigate violence at their establishment.

"We insist." The voice was firm, with a hint of warning. The male looked him squarely in the eyes, and Cal knew better than to reject the offer.

The host dumped the soft female into Cal's lap before offering the opposition's security the next female in line. His female whimpered, and Cal brushed the wavy blonde hair out of her face.

The first thing that stole his breath was her beauty. She was gorgeous, with light grey eyes and little markings all over her face. She had a pert, upturned nose and full, rosy cheeks. The next thing that stole his breath was the myriad of bruises that covered her face and arms.

Anger surged through him. Someone had beaten this small and harmless female black and blue! But Vosken's hand landing on Calix's clenched fist forced Cal to tamp down his anger. He was working, and he needed to keep it together.

He exchanged glances with Vosken before guiding the female to sit between his legs. Cal would have much rather have her curves on his lap, but he knew he needed to keep his wits about him.

She scented heavily of fear, and the scent wrenched a hole in his chest. No female as harmless and soft as the one in front of him should ever be this afraid.

Despite her fear, she robotically reached to open the front of his pants as if she had done it many times. Her actions were from her training, not desire. Cal stopped her. As much as he wanted her hands on him, he wanted her willing and wanting. "I do not need the distraction. I am still working."

She looked thankful and dipped her head.

Unable to stop himself from touching her, Cal petted her, stroking his fingers through the soft, blonde waves, and she relaxed. As her fear subsided, her underlying scent came through. Something was off about it, but it didn't stop Cal from craving her. But from the off smell, Cal knew that she was not his mate. The scent was clear about that. Too bad.

Cal had been looking for his mate for years and had found nothing but meaningless sex and females who were interested in him only for his infamy. They wanted to add the dangerous mercenary to their long list of sexual triumphs. Not one of them had cared about the male beneath.

He was done with casual flings, done with trying to force a mate bond with the wrong person. Or, he had thought he was. After seeing this beauty, he wanted to take every liberty he could with her and then steal her back to his ship to keep forever, even though she was not his mate.

Back on the ship, Cal had endured as all the newly mated couples expressed their love verbally and physically all over the vessel. At least there had been some positive outcomes. One being that Calix had been drinking Vore's Rhean spirits, not that Vore would notice. He was too busy chasing his mate, Lettie, around the ship and celebrating their mating wherever he caught her: on the training mats, in the shared lounge, on the plants in the greenroom, everywhere. Nowhere was safe from the amorous duo.

There were also the other three couples on the ship. His captain, Zeylum, and his mate Ashe were more discreet because Ashe was shy about her sexuality. But Moira and Sidas had always been exhibitionists. And recently, Mia had gotten more comfortable with their sexually expressive culture, so Arus naturally pushed for more. Mia and Lettie were both extremely vocal, and it was hard to find anywhere on the ship to escape their ecstatic cries.

He was happy for his crewmates; they deserved love and ultimate joy. But what about him?

Cal reached for the drink on the table, brought it to his lips, and glugged down a mouthful. The wine was watered down, a far cry from the Rhean spirits he was used to. The establishment wanted their patrons relaxed but not drunk enough to start needless fights.

He tapped on the female's shoulder and handed her the cup. She looked unsure. Cal nodded to her, trying to encourage her to drink. It would help her relax. Cal didn't want her to be stressed.

But she froze as if she was afraid to take the drink from him. Cal held it up to her mouth and tilted it. She took a small sip, and Cal smiled at her in encouragement. She didn't smile back. What would it take to make her smile?

❊ ❊ ❊

Emma was surprised by the muscular Tallean male who directed her to kneel on the floor in front of him. He had gorgeous green eyes and perfect broad shoulders, and when he petted her, running his fingers through her hair, it soothed her. She leaned her head on the alien man's lap, closing her eyes. For a fleeting moment, she felt at peace, and it was utterly at odds with the situation she found herself in.

After being abducted from Earth, Emma'd had three owners. Early on, with her first owner, she had considered fighting and rebelling. But after seeing the results of those who did, Emma decided she'd rather stay alive and with all her fingers and toes. She wanted to be whole when the opportunity for a better life came knocking.

Then she was sold to a breeding facility. It was a quick stint because Emma could not conceive, and therefore was useless to the scientists. Emma went up for auction again, and she was lucky to have been sold to her current owner, a company called the Meeting Ground.

Many merchants and businesses used it as a neutral zone to conduct business and discussions. The females, which they called "distractions," were offered as a luxury, and while it sometimes meant sex, it didn't always end that way. The guards also made sure the patrons were not too rough on their females. The females were, after all, company assets.

So far, this alien was anything but rough with her. The male she was sitting between the legs of was clearly acting security along with the two brawny guards next to him. Even though the Meeting Ground had removed all his weapons, he exuded capability and danger. Emma was sure this alien warrior needed no weapons to be deadly.

Emma looked down at his feet. Like all Talleans, each foot ended in four large claws that stuck out of the front of his boots. His claws were sharp and clean. He wore combat boots with an opening at the front for his claws. The boots had a thick sole, so that when at rest, his claws were held off the ground and out of the dirt.

Sharp fangs poked out of his lips when he smiled. And Emma knew that when he needed to fight a larger opponent, his fangs would fully descend, and the creases on his cheeks would unfold to allow his jaws to unhinge like a monster. Emma had seen those cheek creases in action more than once; Tallean males embraced violence. She had witnessed enough fights to know that the alien who caged her with his legs did not need any weapons. He was the weapon.

And that deadly weapon petted her so gently that she almost forgot she was just a female on loan. Taking a risk, she looked up to inspect his face. She was not supposed to look her clients in the face. He was rough around the edges, not traditionally handsome but rugged and masculine. He wore his dark hair loose just past his shoulders.

It was a unique look for a guard. Many of the males working security wore their hair long and tied back in a ponytail or braided, much like his two friends next to him. Usually, the ones who wore their hair loose were merchants or scholars.

He kept himself clean and tidy, as did his two companions, a rarity for guards. Many of the pant legs she had sat between had been stained with blood and dirt. Her alien guard smelled good too, all clean male and musk, and Emma found herself sniffing at him.

His hand tightened in her hair, and Emma realized that she was sniffing his crotch. She should be embarrassed, but she really didn't have that left in her. She'd done too many things in the past few months to be embarrassed about much anymore.

Besides, this alien would be gone after tonight anyway. Emma would be long forgotten. Why should she be embarrassed? She tried to enjoy this moment of curiosity as much as she could. She would not get it again for a long time, maybe ever.

A hand reached for the liquid-filled cup on the table in front of them, the massive hand dwarfing the container. The alien brought it to his mouth and took a big swig. Then, surprisingly, he tapped her on the shoulder and held the cup to her lips. She wasn't sure what to do. She looked up directly into his face. Gorgeous green eyes met hers, and she froze.

Shit! She wasn't supposed to look the patrons directly in the eyes. She looked away quickly, but he didn't seem upset. Instead, he encouraged her to take the cup.

Emma was suspicious. She'd had one patron give her a drink before, and he had forced her to keep drinking until she was sick. He had laughed as she threw up. The asshole had thought it was funny that humans got sickly drunk on such weak booze. Emma did not want a repeat of that ever again. The manager had been angry with her even though she'd had no other choice. But the owner had heard about it and reprimanded the manager for allowing it to happen. Did he not know that humans could die of alcohol poisoning?

The alien put the cup to her mouth and tilted it. The liquid was cool, and Emma realized she was quite thirsty. She took a small sip. It was light and refreshing. To her relief, he moved the cup away and smiled at her, showing his fangs. She wanted to smile back, but she was too jaded. This man, this male, was being too nice. When something was too good to be true, it often was.

The legs caging her stiffened, and she sat taller, suddenly alert. For the first time, she focused on the deal being discussed at the table. The merchant on their side was selling pirated and illegal ship parts. She didn't understand everything, but it was clear that the other side was unhappy. Unhappy was the wrong word; the other side was furious.

The guard who held her passed her the cup again, urging her to drink. Why did he want her to drink? He had a serious look to his face now, and Emma obeyed, not wanting to upset him.

The thighs tightened around her some more, and a big hand squeezed her shoulder. She now understood why the alien needed to have his wits about him. And it was also only now that she realized that, despite the establishment requiring that all patrons leave their weapons at the door, her alien was still armed. Though compared to the large talons easily accessible on his feet, she wasn't sure what a little knife hidden in his pants would be useful for.

She pressed her hand against the hard knife-shaped outline on his thigh. She looked up at him, and he shot back a wicked grin. Then he took her hand, and he moved it to another location on his body, another weapon. He moved her hand once more as she continued to look into the mesmerizing green of his eyes. Again, her hand landed on something large and rigid. It became obvious after a moment that it was not, in fact, another knife but something a lot more intimate. His body had reacted to her explorations.

Despite having lost all semblance of modesty since being taken from Earth, she felt the heat rise to her face. He smirked at her, licking his lips. But he moved her hand off his crotch to rest back on his thigh before he focused his attention on the tense situation between the two business owners.

Right. He was working. Emma could respect that. Though for the first time since being forced to work here, Emma had wanted to explore the body behind her more intimately.

A bang sounded as a fist hit the table, and a snarl came from the opposing side.

Everything happened so fast, Emma barely had the time to react.

A table flipped over, and the guards on both sides stood at attention.

Emma tried to scramble away as the male who held her stood, but he gripped her wrist and lifted her to standing. He put her behind him and handed her over to one of his friends.

Emma looked up at the brawny alien who now held her by both arms. Unlike the first Tallean, this one looked younger and less experienced. She should get away before things got bad. Emma had heard of females who had bones broken from being stuck under fighting Tallean males. She didn't want to be a statistic. She was already unfortunate enough to be one of those who'd been stolen from Earth. Her track record sucked, and she didn't trust her luck.

Emma pulled away, but the alien held her tight. She tried again, yanking hard, but the other guard next to them added a hand on her shoulder, giving her a tight squeeze. They did not plan on letting her leave.

Something was off. This was not normal behavior. Guards never included the female distraction in their ring of protection. When deliberations broke down, she was either forgotten or thrown aside. They have been taught to run towards the establishment's security when it happened, to avoid injury. That was not an option with her wrists shackled in the guard's large hands.

A fight broke loose. The opposition lunged for the merchant on their side, a knife aimed at his throat. Her alien reacted fast! In a flash, he pulled the attacker off the merchant. They wrestled, but it was clear that her guard was stronger by far, and he soon had the attacker immobilized.

She knew what would happen next. She had witnessed it several times while at the Meeting Grounds working as distraction—the role was aptly named, as the females given to the patrons often distracted the males from fighting.

The well-trained company security rushed in, keeping the disagreeing parties separated. Usually, their job was to keep both clients alive and uninjured until they agreed on a solution, or until one side called off the discussion. But this time, one of the parties had snuck in a weapon and broken the rules of the establishment. Once they broke the rules, their meeting was forfeit. The goal now was to get both parties out of the building with as little damage to company property as possible. The security would now force each party out through separate doors.

The younger guard grabbed her shoulders and pulled her out of the way. A moment later, her alien was back at her side, with her wrist in his hands. She struggled to get out of the big alien's grip, but to no avail. Stuck behind him, with two other guards blocking her, she walked with the group as the security in the establishment pushed the two groups out opposite exits. At five foot six, Emma was hidden from view as the aliens towered over her. Unable to do anything else, she went along.

She looked about wildly. Her alien caught her gaze and sent her a wide, knowing grin. He was stealing her from the Meeting Ground!

Hope flared in her chest. Emma didn't know what life waited for her with this guard turned thief, but she knew she didn't want to stay here. She sure hoped he knew what he was doing!

Pick up a copy to find out what happens!

ALSO BY AUTHOR

TALLEAN MERCENARIES
A Deal for Zeylum
A Chance for Arus
A Promise for Vore
A Claim for Calix
A Minx for Ryek & Holden
A Captive for Kean
A Future for Zharor

TALLEAN MATES NOVELLAS
Becoming Mrs. Claws

XARC'N WARRIORS
Claimed by the Hunter
Wanted by the Hunter
Taken by the Hunter
Cherished by the Hunter

SHORT STORIES

Short stories available through Mailing List only.

Captain Bax's Stowaway

Casch's Runaway Mate

Pursued by the Hunter

Printed in Great Britain
by Amazon